Jerkwater

Jamie Zerndt

Jerkwater

Jamie Zerndt

For Jack Zerndt

CHAPTER ONE
Shawna

THERE WERE SPOTS in the lake where the anchor never hit bottom. The murkiness always fascinated Shawna. She knew it was only tangles of muskgrass and pondweed down there, but a part of her couldn't help but imagine strange, never-before-seen creatures dwelling among the coontails and duckweed. Like Wisconsin anglerfish. Or some rare breed of dwarf whale. And maybe the lake was bottomless, like in those stories her mother used to tell her where Nanaboozhoo was always stumbling and laughing his way through the world.

Shawna dug around inside the cooler. Her journal was peeking out from under a tin of sardines. Ever since the day her stepfather had taken her mother away from her, the journal had become a sort of artificial limb for Shawna. Or maybe an artificial organ, a somewhat bulky and awkward replacement for what had been her heart.

"It's not the world's fault you're lonely," Shawna said out loud. It was something her mother used to say. The words came to her like that sometimes, like ghost ships sailing across the years, reminding her of who her mother had once been: a strong woman who'd been haunted by demons. White demons. Shawna picked up her journal and was sitting with her hand hovering over the page, waiting to take dictation from a dead woman, when she heard the muffled sounds of voices on the water. Then there was the echo of oars being worked in their sockets and a tackle box being slid across a metal hull. She lay flat on the ground, peering through the reeds, and spotted a man rowing quietly toward the island. There was a little boy in the boat, too, a little lump of a thing bundled up in a too-big camouflage coat and looking barely old enough to handle the pole he had dangling over the edge. Then, just as she thought they might row past, the man dropped anchor about forty feet out.

Shawna lowered her head and wondered about *her* boat, if they could see it. As she lay there frozen, she noticed a turtle sunning itself on one of the larger rocks near the island. It was an ugly thing with a head like a wrinkly old penis. The shell, though, was beautiful, almost like the yellow undercoating and the elaborate black hatch-marks were trying to make up for its unflattering head.

"You want me to do it?"

"No. I can do it."

"Then take this one. He's nice and fat."

Shawna couldn't see their faces all that well, but it was definitely them. It was like they were all in the same room together, the walls made of the mist still clinging to the lake. There was the crack of a can opening. Soda maybe. Or beer.

"You hungry?"

"No."

"You sure?"

"I'm sure."

The room became hushed, and Shawna watched the two figures hunched over their rods, waiting. For the man, the waiting seemed like a kind of forced meditation, like something he wasn't all that interested in but that came with the territory of fishing. As for the boy, he didn't seem to want to be there at all. That much Shawna could tell without seeing his face.

"Here." The man handed the boy something. *"Eat."*

"When we get back can we--?"

"Quiet. You've got a bite."

Shawna watched the boy's bobber. There were little ringlets pulsing out from it like sonar. Then nothing.

"I think he ate my worm."

"Maybe. Reel it in a little."

The boy slowly reeled his line in, letting it stop every few feet or so. Then the bobber suddenly disappeared.

"Look!"

"Okay, okay. Let him take it now. That's it."

"Can I reel him in now? Can I?"

"Did you set the hook?"

"I don't know."

"Give it a little tug. Not too hard now."

Shawna could see the boy yank on the line, lifting the pole over his head.

"Jesus, you'll be lucky he still has a mouth left on him." The man went about getting his net ready and leaning over the side of the boat as the boy pulled the fish closer. *"See, I told you this was a good spot. Didn't I tell you?"*

The man lowered the net into the water, but when he brought the fish up, it didn't appear all that big to Shawna. Maybe a bluegill or sunfish. She watched as the boy reached into the net and was sprayed with water as the fish flipped and arched about. The man put the net down on the floor of the boat, no doubt stepping on the fish to keep it from flopping about, then ruffled the boy's hair before carefully pulling the fish from the net and placing it on a stringer. Shawna figured they'd probably go home now, but the boy went back to staring blankly out at the water while the man began casting a bright yellow lure closer and closer to the bank of the island. Shawna guessed he was going for Muskie now since they were known to hide in weed beds. Ojibwa called them *maashkinoozhe.* Or "ugly pike."

"Can we go soon?"

"Soon, Jack."

Shawna knew all too well who they were: Peyton Crane and his little boy. She'd made a sort of hobby over the past year or so of casually stalking them. Lately, though, it had become less casual. She noted the day and time in her journal next to the others.

Something was slid across the hull of the boat. *"Here, have a pretzel. We'll go back soon. I promise."* Peyton stood up in the boat, and Shawna got her first clear look at him.

He was wearing a brown flannel jacket and a camouflage baseball cap, his dumb brown hair sticking out the back like burnt straw. The beer belly pushing out against his flannel made him appear older. And pregnant. Shawna smiled to herself. If that were true, ninety percent of the white men in town would be knocked-up.

Shawna watched as the turtle, apparently having had enough of all the commotion, waddled off his rock and into the water. The turtle reminded her of a story her mother used to tell her about the world being flooded and Nanaboozhoo sitting on a log searching for land. In the story he tried to swim to the bottom of the lake to grab a handful of earth so he could create a new place to live, but the lake seemed bottomless. A loon, a mink, and a turtle also tried to reach the bottom, but all of them failed. Finally, a little muskrat tried. The muskrat didn't survive, but when his lifeless body floated to the surface, they found a ball of earth still clutched in his paw. Nanaboozhoo put the ball on the turtle's back and with the help of the wind from the four directions, the dirt grew into an island which is now North America. Ever since then, Ojibwa have revered the muskrat for his sacrifice, and, also the turtle for literally bearing the weight of the world.

As Shawna daydreamed about the turtle down below holding up the island, she heard something clatter in the branches overhead. There, not a foot away, was a lure with a treble hook swaying and glinting in the sunlight.

"Jesus H. Christ."

Peyton stood up and began yanking on the snagged line, rocking the small boat back and forth so that the boy was forced to set his pole down and grab the oars for support.

"Shit if I'm going to lose another lure to a goddamn tree."

When he eventually gave up and began reeling in the anchor, Shawna pulled the lure down and set the line between her teeth. It took a few bites but soon the lure came free and the line went slack. Shawna could see the boy staring intently at the island, and, for a brief moment, it seemed like they were staring at one another. Almost like the boy had seen what she had done but had decided to remain quiet.

"Look. It came free."

Peyton turned to see his line lying limp and flaccid on the water, and Shawna thought she could see a smile spread across the boy's face.

"You promised we could play video games, 'member?"

Peyton stared hard at the island, like the thought of leaving the lure there somehow meant the island had won.

"Yeah, I remember alright."

He then worked the boat around with one of the oars and began rowing them back across the lake. Shawna rolled over on her back and studied the lure in the sunlight wobbling its way through the leaves. It was a simple lure. Wooden. Handmade. She wondered idly if Peyton had ever caught anything with it. *Save Two Walleyes – Spear A Pregnant Squaw. Too Bad Custer Ran Out Of Bullets.* She remembered the protests and the bumper stickers on the boats from when she was a girl. She remembered, too, the hate white people had spewed at her relatives as they tried to dock with their boats full of walleye. *"Ignorance,"* her mother had told her, *"is a dangerous thing. But now at least you know its face."*

She turned the lure over in her hand, her fingers tracing the lines of the treble hook, pushing the barb gently against her thumb. She found herself thinking about the ceremonies the Plains Indians used to have where the boys pierced their skin with hooks and suspended themselves from chains as a rite of passage. She rested the lure against her shirt, brushing the metal back and forth across the cotton. She wondered how much pain a person could endure. She wondered if enjoying it would somehow invalidate it.

Just as she was imagining her own skin being pulled and stretched, a moth landed on her knee. A gypsy moth. She recognized it because she always thought their floppy antennae made them look like little flying rabbits. They were hated by both whites and Chippewa alike because they were destroying large swaths of Wisconsin forest. It was one of the few things both agreed on. Shawna shooed the moth away, watching as it flitted up into the tree to work its mayhem, and rolled over onto her stomach before tossing the lure into the cooler.

She watched the now tiny boat as it docked along the southern edge of the lake. The poor kid didn't stand a chance. Whether he wanted to be or not, he was a racist-in-training. Half the kid's heart was probably already polluted, and by the time he reached high school, his insides would be entirely black. And what was worse was that things would continue on like that, the kid growing up, having his own kids, and then infecting them. And on and on and on. Like a cancer. Or like a gypsy moth making its home in the family tree. There was nothing for it to do but spread disease.

CHAPTER TWO
Kay

A T SIXTY-FOUR YEARS old, Kay O'Brien found herself half-drunk and sitting inside an old camper wishing her dead husband would emerge from a deepening fog. She angled the flashlight up against the window and pressed the on/off button a few times, scattering a kind of gibberish Morse code out across the lake. In the twilight, the silhouette of the small island resembled a small, hairy elephant. She had been to the island just once before; Norm had taken her in the boat. Just for kicks, he'd said. But there wasn't much to the island, a few trees and a fire pit dug out in the center, the entire length of the island no more than twenty feet long, barely enough room for a couple of sleeping bags. A person could live on it, she supposed, but who'd want to?

The Scamp had rolled down the hill years ago, coming to rest against a stand of paper birch along the edge of the lake where it has stayed ever since. Kay sat in the back of the small camper, near the window closest the water, staring out at the foam on the lake. A noise had brought her out of the house, a yelling of some sort. That's when she noticed the boat was missing. Douglas couldn't have taken it out because he'd only just left for *Ruggers*. And even though she knew it wasn't possible, a part of her couldn't stop from hoping that maybe Norm *was* out there.

Earlier, when she'd found the neighbor girl's horse wandering around their backyard, she'd tied him to the old tin fishing shack near the dock. The girl must have forgotten to corral him. Either that or she was out on the island. Seven was a monster of an animal. One hoof from him and Kay would be done for. A mercy, perhaps, at this point, but still the beast awed her. Just the way its muscles twitched and rippled whenever it took a step was enough to put Kay into a sort of trance. Never in her life, except for maybe when Douglas was born, had she stared at another human being with that same depth of wonder and appreciation.

She fooled with the flashlight again, moving the beam across the water, hoping to catch a glimpse of what? An apparition of some sort? Or maybe the Loch Ness monster? She wondered for a moment what the monster would be called if she did find one. *The Little Pike Lake Monster*. Not exactly the stuff of legends. Kay waited and listened to the bleating of bullfrogs and crickets, the blustering and snorting of Seven. On the counter was a sketchbook of her son's. Douglas had been spending more and more time in the camper since his father had died. She left him alone for the most part, but there were times like these when she couldn't help but do a little snooping. She flipped through the sketches slowly, like she was reading a diary. What made her sad was that the only other audience for them were the weevils and roly-polys infesting the old camper. And soon there wouldn't even be Kay. Not really anyway. The Alzheimer's diagnosis had come only months after Norm died. She hadn't even told Douglas yet. The poor kid had enough on his plate.

She looked out at the water again and thought she could see the dark outline of a boat gliding toward the dock. With the fog, the oar sticking up resembled a scythe, like Death itself were floating across the water toward her. She set the sketchbook down, leaving it just as she'd found it, open to a slightly disturbing sketch of a loon with a broken neck, and went outside to wait alongside Seven.

"You like me a little bit, don't you?" Kay whispered and stroked the coarse hairs on the animal's great neck as he began to lightly stamp and hoof at the ground. The boat, it turned out, was real and gliding straight for their dock. Again Kay caught herself waiting for Norm to come into view, holding up a fat bluegill for her to praise. She switched on the flashlight and this time caught a flesh-and-blood person in the beam: the girl from next door.

"Shawna? That you out there caterwauling?" Kay called out as the girl clipped the johnboat to one of the steel rings along the edge of the dock. As Kay stood studying her, something about the way the girl hugged her sweatshirt tight against herself made Kay think she'd been swimming out there. But when Shawna came closer, she noticed there wasn't a drop of water on her.

"You okay?"

"I guess."

The girl silently greeted the horse, her hand on his nose, the two of them as familiar with one another as an old married couple.

"You're trembling," Kay said.

"It's cold out."

"Not *that* cold."

There was another noise, another oar working away at the water out there. Kay considered getting the flashlight out again but thought better of it. It was none of her business who the girl had been with.

"That boat I'm pretending not to hear the reason you're borrowing mine?"

Shawna nodded. "My naan thinks I'm at a girlfriend's house." She began to untie the horse. "It's just some boy I'm seeing. It's nothing. Nothing important enough to tell anybody about anyway."

Kay stared at the girl. She was far from all right. Just about a canter away from very much not alright. "It sounded pretty important to me. Important enough for it to interrupt my show."

Again the girl busied herself with the horse, looking everywhere but at Kay. She'd make a good boxer, ducking and weaving the way she did.

"Come inside and have a beer with me."

"Is Douglas home?"

"Out drinking with Marty."

"I can't stand Marty."

"Marty's okay. He's just a little confused sometimes. C'mon, we'll steal some of Douglas's Leineys."

Kay, not bothering to wait for a response, started up the hill using the old walking stick her husband had carved for her. Lately, she found herself using the cane more and more. Even on flat ground she was feeling a little off-balance these days. Like the very ground beneath her was moving, the world tilting imperceptibly. The cane did help a little, but for how much longer she wasn't sure.

Kay left the screen door open and went rummaging through the fridge for a beer, but there were none left. "Because you weren't any fun," she said out loud as she began making a Manhattan for herself, and another, smaller one, for Shawna.

"Who are you talking to?"

"Was I talking? I was, wasn't I?"

"You said somebody wasn't fun."

"Sorry. Just finishing a conversation I was having in my head. My Norm was asking why I never drank much when he was alive. Here," Kay said and handed the girl a drink. "This will have to do. Looks like we're skint in the beer department."

"Skint?" Shawna said, taking a seat at the kitchen table.

"Broke. Busted. What I mean is we've got no beer."

The drink in front of Kay was Norm size, big enough to sedate a horse. "You may find this hard to believe, but I never used to drink much. Not like this, anyway. I'd have a small one here and there, but that's all I ever wanted. I didn't need it. I was busy. I had my family around me." Kay picked up the glass, swirled it so that the cubes jostled and then settled back alongside one another. "I guess maybe now I do need it."

"It's okay," Shawna said quietly. "I get that."

Kay looked at the girl. She *did* get it. Sometimes Kay forgot about the girl's mother, about what happened, but never for very long. They sat in silence for a bit until Shawna asked to use the bathroom. After the girl had left, Kay sat alone at the table listening as the bathroom fan started up. Norm could be in there, maybe showering before bed. She would never tell anybody this, but sometimes she took the cap off his shaving cream and smelled it. *Barbasol.* It was a silly thing to do, but it brought him back for a brief moment. He was like an echo in the house now, something she could sometimes hear but could never find the source of.

When Shawna returned, Kay watched as she took a sip of her drink and grimaced. "This is horrible. Thank you."

Kay laughed. "It's an old person's drink. A Manhattan. I don't suppose you've ever had one before."

"I've never even heard of it before."

They sat staring out at the darkening lake for a bit while the girl nursed her drink. Kay knew that if she pushed the girl too hard, she'd spook. Even so... "Am I still not supposed to ask about the boy or do you maybe want to talk about it now? I'm an old woman, could fall over any second. I don't have much time for small talk."

Kay followed the girl's eyes as she took in the pile of dirty dishes on the countertop, the garbage overflowing in the can. Kay helped herself to a nice, long sip of her drink. It felt like somebody had poured the very spark and glow of life into her glass, but she knew there'd be hooks attached to it come morning.

"I know," Kay said, more to her drink than to the girl, "I've turned into a pig." She raised her glass. "Here's to tomorrow. Here's to clean dishes."

Shawna nodded, then raised her glass and took a drink.

"You don't have to answer this if you don't want to," Kay went on, "but I'm guessing you go out there to have sex."

Shawna shrugged. "Sometimes. Yeah."

It wasn't the answer Kay had expected. She wondered how much sex Douglas was having, if any. She didn't give it much thought most of the time. Which would probably be different if she'd had a girl. "Did you tell that boy out there no tonight? Is that why he was yelling?"

"No," Shawna said, leaning back in her chair. "That was me you heard."

"Oh." Kay watched the girl and it seemed to her now that she was all hard lines. She thought about how they say if you see a straight line in nature then you know it's man-made. And if anything was man-made, it was this girl sitting across from her. "Did you two have a fight?"

"No. It wasn't anything like that."

"Then what was it?"

"Just letting off some steam."

"You angry at anything in particular?"

"The world?"

"Well, join the club. Most people are angry at the world."

"The *white* world."

"Oh," Kay said and set her drink down. "That's something different then, isn't it?"

"For you maybe."

"Fair enough."

Kay waited as Shawna stared out the window some more. Both the lake and the window were engulfed in black now, only the yellow kitchen light reflecting back. Even so, the girl sat with her chin in her hand, her long black hair hiding most of her face. It looked safe to Kay. Comfortable. She herself had once had long hair, but it was so long ago now she couldn't remember how it had felt. A part of her wanted to reach out and stroke the girl's hair, feel it in her hands, smell it even. She bet it smelled of light and air and outside. She looked at the veins on the back of her hand as she clutched the half-empty tumbler in front of her. She hardly ever noticed them anymore, the veins, but now, for whatever reason, they stood out. Big blue snakes burrowing under blotted skin, skin that belonged to a stranger, to her mother before she died. None of this, the house, the girl, the lake, none of it was Kay. Kay was not the blue snake. Kay was not the skin she could stretch like silly putty. Kay wasn't any of these things. Kay was this young girl's hair.

"Elmer got the shit kicked out of him recently."

"And Elmer's the boy on the island?"

"Yeah. He's still in high school, though."

"He goes to Mercer High?"

"Yep. He's a senior. We just have to make it to next year."

"And what happens next year?"

The girl eyed her, cautious as a cat. "We move. To Madison. Further maybe."

"And what's in Madison?"

"Nothing." Again she hesitated, then, like once again she'd decided Kay was okay, added, "Or maybe veterinary school."

"Douglas mentioned that. Did you get in?"

"I just found out. But it wouldn't start until next year."

"Well, congrats, young lady. That's a pretty big deal." The girl shrugged, but Kay could see a smile trying to get out behind that hair of hers. "So what would this Elmer be doing in Madison?"

"Paying our rent."

Kay laughed. "Sounds like you got it all figured out."

"Not really. It's just something to think about."

"Can I ask why he's getting hurt at school? Is it because he's Native American?"

"No," Shawna said, pushing the hair back from her face and looking at Kay. "It's because he's an Indian."

Occasionally Kay heard comments after church, or at the grocery store while standing in line, little whispers here and there about how the Indians were taking all the fish or getting into trouble with the law, but she had rarely seen any outright abuse. Still, she knew it was there, simmering just beneath the surface of the town.

"I hate this goddamned town sometimes. I really do."

The girl shrugged and, for a brief moment, looked just like any other typical teenager. "It's just that lately it's been getting bad. Elmer is strong, but he can't handle two of them at once. It just isn't fair. And he won't ever back down. He's too proud."

Kay wriggled a couple fingers, causing the largest blue snake to writhe. "They say the biggest branch either bends in the storm or it breaks." It was something Norm had said to her once. He was grumbling about having to do something he didn't want to around the house, but Kay had never forgotten the line. When she asked him where he heard it, he said he thought it was from Buddha. It was only sometime later that he admitted he'd read it on a bathroom wall somewhere. Which, for whatever reason, had only made Kay appreciate the phrase all that much more.

Shawna looked down at her glass, letting her hair fall back into her face. "We've been bending for a long time now. You bend too much, you'll snap anyway, right?"

Kay smiled at the girl. "You're one smart lady, you know that?"

Again, the girl shrugged. They spoke some more about what was going on with Elmer, how he seemed to attract trouble because he was big and quiet and there were always boys who wanted to test themselves against him or needed to prove something. Then Shawna, her voice hollow, like she was speaking from somewhere deep inside herself, said, "Do you ever think about what your life would have been like if you still lived back wherever your people are from? Sometimes I wonder if I'd think about that if I were a white person. Or if I wouldn't care at all. I guess what I'm saying is sometimes I wonder what kind of white person I'd be."

Kay didn't know what to say. "Ireland," she said finally.

"My maiden name is Farrell, so that's where I'd probably be."

"So both you and your husband are Irish?"

"In name only really. But, yes, just a coincidence."

"Maybe."

"What does that mean?"

"Same tribe is all. Anyway, I heard that place is like one big white rez."

Kay laughed. "I don't know. I've never been."

"Really? I can't imagine not knowing where I came from. Even if it *is* just a shithole." Shawna looked up. "I meant Lac du Flambeau. Not Ireland, necessarily."

"It's okay. I know what you meant." Kay took a sip of her Manhattan and looked at the girl, at the seeming thickness of her skin, at how adeptly it hid all the pain she knew was there under it. "Can I ask you something?"

"We use protection. We're not stupid."

"No, no, nothing like that. But good. That's good."

"Sorry. Did I embarrass you?"

"I'm 64 years old. I don't get embarrassed."

The girl smiled a touch. "So are you going to ask your question or what?"

"No. I don't think so."

Shawna shook her head. "I think maybe you're a little drunk."

"I think maybe you're a little right."

Kay watched as the girl sipped at her drink, watched as she winced and the corners of her eyes squeezed tight.

There was a deep anger burning inside the girl. How, after everything that had happened, could there not be?

Kay raised her glass. "To humanity. To all the limburger cheeses in the world."

"Limburger?"

"It's something my Norm used to say. He liked to think of people as different kinds of cheeses. The limburgers of the world were an acquired taste."

"So what kind was he?"

"Limburger."

"And you?"

Kay watched the mosquitoes pinging off the porch light outside. Somewhere a loon called.

Somewhere a loon was always calling.

"Norman said I was a porcupine ball. Spiky on the outside but with a little something for everyone."

"That's good then."

"You ever seen one?"

"No."

"They're not exactly pretty."

Shawna wiped at her mouth with a napkin. There were blue flowers on the napkins. Morning Glories. Kay hadn't ever really noticed the print before. It bothered her for some reason. They were old-lady napkins. If she wasn't careful, soon she'd be putting out hard candies.

"I should be getting back home. My naan will worry."

Kay nodded. "Just a few more minutes, okay? I want to show you something." Kay, trying her best not to groan too much as she stood from the table, went into the living room. When she returned, she handed the girl a small wooden box. "Here lies Limburger cheese."

Shawna took the box from her and set it on the table, one hand resting on it as one might rest a hand upon a purring cat. "This isn't a good place for him."

"No, maybe not, but it's a good place for me. I like having him close, silly as that may sound."

"Can I tell you something and you promise not to tell Douglas?"

"I promise."

"Sometimes I can hear my mom talking to me. And it's not like a whisper or anything. I can actually *hear* her. Like she's standing right next to me. Do you think that's messed up?"

"Well, if it is," Kay said, "I guess that means I'm messed up, too."

As she looked across the table at Shawna, she could clearly remember holding her mother's hand as she lay dying, the spaces getting longer and longer between breaths, only for the old woman to somehow resurface and suck in yet another long, ragged breath. Kay had heard stories of Indians letting their elderly walk out in the woods without any food or water to die. They went out in the open, under the sky, listening to the wind rather than the ridiculous chatter of humans. Kay's world seemed so soft and easy in comparison.

"You know what I had for lunch today?" Kay finally said. "A can of beef stew. But these here, these are all recipes of mine." She tapped a tin can resting in the middle of the table. "Some handed down to me by my mother. There's a decent lasagna, pot roasts, a meatloaf, that sort of thing. I never really liked my mom, though. That's the God's honest truth. When she died, I don't even think I cried." Kay waved her hand in the air, like she was trying to shoo away what she'd just said. "But these recipes, you know what's funny? I made these meals for Douglas and Norm for years and years and now I can't remember eating any of it. The cooking, sure, I can remember that. But not the eating. I don't know. Something about that doesn't seem right."

Shawna pushed her glass away. "I hate meatloaf."

Kay liked how the girl didn't smile much, how she wore flannels and jeans and Doc Martin boots. She knew they were Doc Martin's because Douglas had asked for a pair his sophomore year. "I don't suppose I could talk you into marrying my son someday."

"I don't date white boys."

"Isn't that racist?"

"I'm pretty sure I get a pass on that."

When Shawna and her horse eventually sauntered off down the road, something about it reminded Kay of one of those poems they were always reading on NPR that she could never quite understand. Or like all that much. Only this poem was floating out there on the dark, the girl herself like a mysterious line held in the hands of the old, weathered road.

Kay made sure to leave the porch light on in case Douglas showed up later and then went about getting ready for bed. The mere sight of her son's towel on the rack took some of the empty out of the house. When she lay down on her side of the bed, the left side, she knew she probably wouldn't be able to sleep any time soon. Sometimes, in the middle of the night, she found herself on Norm's side of the bed, her arm resting atop a cold pillow. She'd considered buying a new bed at one point, something smaller perhaps, but she knew she'd never be able to go through with it. Besides, their bed had never been all that big to begin with. They'd always liked sleeping beside one another; there'd never been any real need for something larger.

Once settled, Kay lay awake listening to the loons. What strange creatures they were. Long ago, they used to serve as a sort of bookmark to her days, reminding her to be thankful, to stop and take notice of the good things in her life. But the loons did something else to her now: they reminded her of her loneliness. Kay turned off the lamp and rolled over on her side, giving herself over to the howling of the strange birds. As she tried to sleep, she found herself thinking of hairy elephants wading out into the dark lake and then grimacing at the question she'd nearly asked Shawna. Had she seriously been about to ask if Ojibwa people ate loons? She buried her head in the pillow, her eyes wide open, realizing she'd forgotten to give the girl the tin of recipes like she'd planned.

CHAPTER THREE
Douglas

"You know what Ojibwa think happens when a person dies?"

This was typical Shawna. No messing around, straight to the point. And that point was Douglas's dad. Douglas had found him in the backyard, face down, his fishing rod out in front of him like he was trying to cast his way back up the hill to salvation. And the worst thing about it all was that his dad had asked him just a few weeks before to put in the steps. But Douglas never had. Until now. He kicked his shovel into the dirt and used the bottom of his shirt to wipe at the sweat dripping into his eyes as Shawna and Seven watched.

"I don't know," he forced himself to say. "What?"

"They say your spirit enters the body of a large animal and then travels down into smaller and smaller ones until it disappears."

"Disappears where?"

"Into the next world."

"And you believe that?"

"Sure, why not? Seems just as likely as your halos and pitchforks."

"I don't believe in that stuff either, so..."

"So it's just something to think about," Shawna said. "I like the idea of it anyway."

Then Douglas said something he found himself saying a lot lately. Something he knew was stupid, but it was like he couldn't help himself. "My dad died."

Good fishing today, eh, Douglas? : My dad died.

How 'bout them Packers? : My dad died.

That'll be $14.97. : My dad died.

"Who knows," Shawna said, ignoring him. "Maybe his spirit is hiding out in the Loon."

"Not funny."

Shawna jerked the reins so Seven couldn't leave the conversation. "No, I guess not. Sorry."

Douglas shrugged, kicking down on the shovel again. "The weird thing is I keep thinking he's going to stroll into the shop one day, tell me how I'm screwing everything up."

Douglas's dad owned an auto repair shop in town called Norm's. Which Douglas was now running. Into the ground, if things didn't pick up soon.

Shawna tilted her head, scooping her hair to the side and tucking it behind her ear. "I am sorry about your dad, Douglas."

Douglas stared at the horse's nostrils, at how they

contracted in and out like a heart. Before he could think of anything more to say, Seven sidestepped away, almost like he was annoyed with Douglas for staring.

"Me, too," he finally managed to say, and Shawna nodded, like she could hear the lack of conviction in his voice and understood it. The three of them stared at the lake, at the wind blowing across the surface. The small waves pushing across the water reminded Douglas of a blanket being shaken out in slow motion.

"See you then," Shawna said after a bit, she and Seven turning as one and clomping off down the road again.

Douglas had no right to feel sorry for himself in front of her, not after what had happened to her mother. After the funeral, Shawna's naan had no choice but to move in with Shawna. She'd bought her Seven shortly after that, and the two had been inseparable ever since.

Douglas went back to digging even though there was no real point now. At the bottom of the hill, his dad's old tin fishing shack moaned in the wind like it was begging to be put out of its misery. But the shack would stay. Everything stayed for now. That was the unspoken agreement between Douglas and his mother: they touched nothing.

———

THE NEXT DAY Shawna stopped by and asked if Douglas wanted to check out the new coffee shop. They'd never had a real coffee shop in Mercer before. Not unless you counted the bait shop which proudly advertised its combo deals on espresso shots and night crawlers.

They didn't talk much on the way there, the sun acting like a thumb flipping through the pages of trees as they drove. It was something Douglas loved about the UP, the way it could sometimes put you in a trance.

When they entered The Fresh Pot, the first thing they noticed were the oil paintings on the walls. Not only were there no images of the standard deer, elk, or monster-sized northern pike on the wall, there wasn't a single loon in the place either. The holiest of Mercer holies: missing.

"What do you think?" Douglas asked as they stared at what he already considered masterpieces.

Shawna was looking at a painting of somebody bearing an uncanny resemblance to George Bush. He was wearing a Hitler-esque mustache and had a small oil rig protruding from his pants. It was a geyser, the oil fairly leaping off the canvas.

"Maybe nobody told her she moved to Bushville, Wisconsin," Shawna said, still eyeing George's fly.

The painting beside it was of the Pope water skiing in the Wisconsin Dells with six petrified-looking altar boys. Then there was another of a futuristic McDonald's with two drive-thrus: one for food, the other for gastric-bypass surgery. The owner was sitting behind the counter reading a copy of *The New Yorker*. She was skinny, her arms covered in colorful tattoos, her hair dyed a metallic red and pulled back in a bun. The t-shirt she was wearing had a drawing of the Millennium Falcon on it. Douglas figured she was in her thirties, even though she dressed a lot younger than that.

"Did you paint these?" Douglas asked after they put their orders in.

"Why? Do you like them?"

"Yeah. A lot."

"Well, in that case, yes, I painted them."

Shawna stuck out her hand when Douglas went quiet and began staring at the countertop. "I'm Shawna. And this is Douglas. He's an artist, too."

"Jenna," the woman said and shook hands with both of them. She then went about making the drinks, a cloud of steam rising up so that she was forced to turn her head away. Something about it, the twist of her neck maybe, made Douglas's stomach flutter. "I bet Douglas here is a pretty good artist. You know how I know?"

"How?" Shawna said, taking her drink.

"Because he doesn't look like an artist. From my experience, that's usually a good sign. You should bring something in some time and show me. Eventually I'll be needing new work to put up. That is, if I don't go out of business by then."

Shawna gave Douglas a little nudge when he didn't say anything. "Yeah," he muttered, "I'll do that. For sure."

They went and sat by the front window, and almost immediately Shawna leaned over, whispered, "Did you notice the nipple rings?"

"No."

"Yes, you did. You can totally see." But when Shawna

saw him turning around, she placed a hand on his arm. "Don't look now. Do it on the way out if you have to."

"It must've hurt."

"I think that's the whole point. Pleasure and pain, all that."

"Oh."

Outside, a line of cars waited at the stoplight. One of the bumper stickers read *Wife and Dog Missing: Reward for Dog*. "I fucking hate this jerkwater town," Shawna said, nodding toward the car. "My favorite so far has to be *Save a Walleye, Spear a Squaw*."

The cars moved off through the intersection like a lazy herd of deer. "Yeah, I think Marty might have one of those on the back of his sled."

Marty had worked down at the shop with Douglas ever since high school. They'd all graduated a few years back, but so far none of them had gotten around to going to college. Which wasn't really even much of a real possibility for Marty, not unless they had a university for fishing somewhere nearby.

"Did I ever tell you about the time we were holding a ceremony out on the Flambeau and these people started throwing beer cans at us? They kept telling us to go home. You know what that's like? That's like me walking into your house and telling you to go home."

Douglas couldn't help but wonder if Marty had been there. Maybe. But he couldn't see him throwing cans. *Hate in a can*. That's what people called Treaty Beer. Some local's idea of a statement. People said it was about the fishing rights, but it wasn't really. People caught plenty enough fish. It was because they were Indians. Simple as that. Fishing rights was just something they could cover their hate up with.

"Mom said something about you screaming out on the island the other night. That true?"

"It was more like howling, but, yeah, guilty."

"I feel like that sometimes."

"Because of your dad?"

"Yeah."

Shawna stared at her coffee for a bit, then, watching what little traffic there was, said, "You ever get cut off by somebody and maybe you even almost go off the road because of it and then they stick their hand out the window and give you the finger right before they get off an exit? Like it's too late to yell at them or anything because they're already gone and you'll never see them again?"

"Yeah, I guess."

"That's what death can feel like. There's no one to take it out on because they're gone. Or in my case, they're in prison."

Douglas, not sure what to say to this, mumbled, "You still thinking about vet school?"

"I am. I actually got in believe it or not."

"No shit? You going to go?"

"Nah, I thought I'd keep working at the casino because I love watching white people throw their money away."

"Seriously."

"Yeah, probably. I still need to talk to my naan about it. She'll have to come with me. I wouldn't go without her."

"Good. That's good."

"What about you? You going to spend your life hanging out with Marty in that grease pit?"

"I have to take care of the shop. And my mom."

"Your mom can take care of herself."

"Maybe. Maybe not."

Later, as they left, Douglas stole one last look at Jenna. She was like one of the paintings on the wall: something that didn't quite fit in with the rest of the town. And he liked that. A lot.

When he dropped Shawna back off at home, she told him about a protest they were holding outside The Wampum Shop the next day. Something to do with Treaty Beer.

"Working," Douglas muttered, hoping she'd leave it alone.

"But it's just across the street from you."

"We're pretty backed up, Shawna. I mean, it's not like I can just--"

"Yeah," Shawna said without letting him finish. "I get it. Not so great for business probably."

As she walked away, it seemed to Douglas like her voice was still hanging there in the air around him. Almost like a dark cloud. There was something new, too, in the way her mood seemed to shift in the space of a breath. It worried him. It was like being able to recognize your own darkness in another's. Only this darkness was an entirely different species than his own. Charcoal vs. pencil. Smoke vs. fire.

EVER SINCE NORM died, Marty had gotten into the habit of picking up tools around the shop and sighing over them. Sometimes Douglas thought Marty missed his dad more than he did. But Douglas lived in a house full of reminders, so a hydraulic jack didn't faze him all that much these days.

"You hear about that drunk-ass Indian?" Marty said, rolling a socket wrench in the palm of his hand. It was a Saturday. They were at the shop replacing someone's alternator.

"Nope."

"I guess one of them tried holding up the Quickie Mart with an iPhone."

"And?"

"It's just typical is all I'm saying. Bunch of freaking morons."

"You ever think how The Wampum Shop is run by a white woman?" Douglas said as calmly as possible. "All these tourists stopping to buy tom-toms. Or, if they're feeling a little crazy, maybe a dream catcher or two."

"Hell," Marty said, flipping the wrench end over end. "They're free to open up their own stores and call them Whitey's if they want."

Douglas was all too familiar with Marty's take on the subject. He knew his only option, if he wanted to finish the car in any kind of peace, was to ignore him. Which he did. But, later, when he was filling out the paperwork, Marty came into the office holding a wooden statue of Don Quixote seasoned with years of grease.

"You going to keep ol' Don around?"

"I don't know," Douglas said. "With all these drunk Indians running around, maybe we could use him to protect the shop."

"Very funny. Where'd Norm get him anyway?"

"Spain, I think. He told me he got it off some street vendor."

"I always thought Cervantes was a type of champagne," Marty said and placed the statue on the desk. "Anyway, I just thought you might want to take him home. Or if you didn't, you know, maybe I could."

"I think Norm would have liked him to stay in the shop. I still have his fishing rod, though, if you want."

"No, that wouldn't be--"

"Marty, you know how often I fish."

"Yeah, angler of the frickin' year."

"Exactly. I'll bring it in one day. Meantime, why don't you see if you can't get those brake lines bled. After that, we can check out the protest."

"Pass," he said and started to leave.

"You know there's a sign over the bar at Old 51 that says *No Red Niggers*. Still think there isn't a problem?"

"Oh, come off it. They lost."

"Lost what?"

"The war. I suppose you think we should send Christmas cards to the Japs and Nazis, too?"

"I didn't know you could win a genocide."

"Whatever. Even your Dad used to say they should call themselves the Chippa-wah-wahs since they're always crying about something."

"Just forget I asked."

"Consider it forgotten," Marty said, grabbing the statue by the neck. "I'll put the champagne back by the oil."

ABOUT TWO DOZEN people, all Chippewa, dressed in jeans and t-shirts, walked up and down the sidewalk outside The Wampum Shop. Shawna held a sign that read *Don't Honor The Treaty Beer!*

"Shouldn't they be dressed up, wearing feathers or something?" Marty said, taking a pull from his Big Gulp like he was at a parade. He'd changed his mind about watching after Douglas told him he wouldn't have to clock out.

"How should I know?"

"Thought you were the expert."

"I'm going over to say hi to Shawna."

"You think that's a good idea?"

"What? Afraid I'll get scalped?"

Outside The Wampum Shop, there was one of those

cigar-store Indians, only now the face was covered with a blown-up photo of the Treaty Beer owner.

"You sure you want to be here?" Shawna said, stepping out from the circle of protestors. She had something yellow and silver dangling from her ear that looked like an old fishing lure.

"Yeah," Douglas said, trying not to stare at her new choice of jewelry. "Why not?"

She nodded toward Marty. "What will your friend over there think?"

"Think? Not much fear of that happening."

Shawna, lowering both her sign and her voice, said, "The owner is kind of freaking out." She leaned closer and went into an over-the-top Wisconsin accent. *"Youz guys better get goin' dare or I'm gonna hafta call da police now, 'kay."*

Douglas was about to say something about the owner, Maggie, when there was something like an explosion behind them. At first Douglas thought maybe there'd been a car accident, but then he turned and realized what had happened. For a few seconds, nobody moved, and he and Shawna just stared at the place where The Wampum Shop's front window used to be.

"What the hell was that?" Shawna kicked at a can of Treaty Beer foaming on the ground. "You have to be kidding me."

A car had driven past and was nearly out of sight. The owner was now screaming inside the shop, no doubt convinced one of the protestors was to blame. Douglas's dad would know what to do here. He'd place a gentle hand on the right shoulder, make things dissolve without ever seeming to lift a finger. But Douglas wasn't his father. Not even close. Unsure of what to do, he went to get a broom from the shop to help clean up. When he got back, a Mercer patrol car with a picture of a loon wearing sunglasses on its door was already parked in the street. And, to make matters worse, Marty was walking over.

"It came from our side," Marty said, his hands in his pockets as he stared at the can still hemorrhaging on the sidewalk.

"You sure?" The officer nudged the can with his boot like he was checking to make sure it was dead. Officer Christopher. Somebody both Douglas and Marty had gone to high school with. He was a tool back then, too.

"Well, I sure didn't do it." Marty looked over at Shawna like she'd just accused him of something. "Peyton threw it."

The officers gave each other a look. They knew exactly who Marty was talking about. Peyton Crane. The guy behind Treaty Beer.

"He hucked it out his car window," Marty said. "I saw him. Everyone did."

"We need to get a statement from you."

"No way."

"You just told us you saw--"

"Sorry," Marty mumbled, heading back to the shop. "I can't right now."

WHEN HE GOT home, Douglas poked his head into the living room and found his mom talking to a small wooden box. He went back into the kitchen, banging around more than he needed to, and by the time he finally made his way into the living room again, his father's urn was back on top of the TV.

"A little early, isn't it?" Douglas said, eyeing his mom's drink.

"It's raining out. What else am I supposed to do?"

Now that she had decided to start drinking like Norm, she made her Manhattans in the same huge tumbler he used to. They held about three of whatever a normal person would drink.

"Hold on," Douglas said. "I'll have one, too."

Drinks in hand, they flipped between sitcoms and old movies, never staying on one channel for more than a few minutes. This was a strange, new freedom for them. Norm had been a dictator when it came to the TV. Now that he was gone, there was almost a guilty thrill in skipping past The History Channel.

"I see you're spending some time with Shawna," his mom said. "That's good."

"Yeah. It's okay."

She took a healthy sip of her drink. "You do realize your odds of dating her are about as good as catching a Muskie."

"I don't fish."

"All men fish."

"Stop."

"I just don't like seeing you torture yourself, honey."

"I know you'll find this hard to believe, but I'm really not interested in her. We're just friends."

His mom waved her drink in the air, dismissing the subject, and they settled on an episode of *Matlock*. *"I sure do love shrimp,"* Matlock said in his rumpled white polyester suit and then raised his bushy eyebrows so everybody knew he'd just figured out who the murderer was. *"Shrimp! That's it!"* he said, just in case they somehow missed it.

Douglas turned the volume down. "Didn't he, like, beat his wife or something?"

"You're thinking of Bing Crosby. It was his kids, I think."

"I bet they both did."

"Probably. They're all assholes once the cameras are off. Except for Cary Grant. He was one of the good ones."

"To Cary Grant."

They toasted and watched as Matlock disappeared behind another commercial, then Douglas turned the volume up and they went back to more flipping.

CHAPTER FOUR
Shawna

S ITTING ON HER back porch, Shawna's entire body hummed. She felt numb, but there was also a sharpness to everything. A clarity. She used an old pair of binoculars to track when Peyton Crane's lights went on and off, when he went fishing, when his boy was over. Tonight the lights were all on, his bulky figure passing by the window every ten minutes or so, no doubt stumbling his dumb way to the fridge for more crappy beer. It gave her hatred a target. And somehow just knowing he was in reach, that at any second she could stand up and give into everything that had been slow-cooking inside, calmed her. It was in this charged calm, watching the moths slam-dance around the porchlight, that she saw Douglas sitting out on the dock in the moonlight, plucking at the ropes on his dad's old bait box.

She walked down and nodding at the half-rack of Treaty Beer by his side, said, "That what I think it is?"

"It is." He handed her one. "Marty bought them as a joke."

"Hilarious." She sat down beside him, grabbed one. "You just getting home?"

"Yep." Douglas reached down, trying to heft the bait box up out of the water, but it was too heavy. "It's weird not seeing any fish in there. I bet the fish threw a party when they found out he died. When I was a kid, I'd come home after school and find maybe half-a-dozen sunfish floating in here." He untied the ropes leashing it to the dock. "Give me a hand with this, will you?"

Shawna stood, grabbing one of the ropes, and together they lifted it out of the water. "What are we doing?"

"It deserves a proper burial," Douglas said and started to sway the chicken-wire box back and forth between them. "On three, okay?"

When they launched the thing off the dock, though, it only made it a couple of feet out.

"I can still see it," Shawna said, trying not to laugh. Half of the box was still sticking out of the water.

They sat down again, drinking and watching like maybe it would sink, but it never did budge. When Shawna started tapping the top of the water with her shoe, Douglas asked what was bothering her.

"Who said anything was bothering me?"

"Your feet did."

"Whatever." Shawna studied the rings pulsing out around her shoe. "I'm just tired of it all, tired of sitting here watching Peyton Crane live his happy life. Maybe it's time I sent a message."

"Okay," Douglas said. "And how exactly do we do that?"

"We?"

"Yeah. We."

Shawna took a drink, grimaced. "Come with if you want, but you won't like it."

"Come with where?"

"You'll see," she said, and the tapping stopped. "We're going to do a little fishing. Ojibwa-style."

Shawna left Douglas on the dock, returning a few minutes later with a duffle bag she'd prepared weeks ago.

"We going to spear fish?" Douglas said, half-kidding.

"Something like that."

Once they were afloat in Norm's john boat, Shawna took out a bag of tobacco and laid some on top of the water. She then pulled a helmet with a car headlight mounted on it from the bag and placed it on her head. She connected it to a car battery at her feet.

"It's how we find the walleye," she said. "Disappointed?"

"Not even a little."

"Good. Because we're not hunting walleye."

Shawna scanned the mud flats along the bank. The walleye were there, huddled just beneath the surface, the light reflecting off their eyes as her helmet flamed away.

"Then what are we doing?"

"Counting coup," Shawna said and aimed the light to

where she wanted Douglas to paddle. Soon they were on the other side of the lake in front of a small house. There was a truck in the driveway, toys in the yard. On the dock sat a child's lunchbox. Shawna's lamp came to a stop, and the light stayed frozen there. She could just make out the word *Spider-Man* on the front of the lunchbox, the red of a costume pushing through rust.

"I had one of those as a kid," Shawna said, killing the light. "My mom bought it for me. My naan always teased me, said our people had our own heroes, our own stories. I kept it secret after that, had to hide all my comics under my mattress. Mom never cared though. She said heroes came from all sorts of different places."

Her mother had married a white man. That had been her first mistake. Shawna's real father had bailed when Shawna was just four. Last she heard he was living on a Hopi reservation in Arizona, re-married to someone who liked to drink and fight just as much as he did. Her own mother never touched the stuff. Which Shawna always found strange as she seemed attracted to men who seemed to do nothing *but* touch the stuff. But all men had liked her mother. She was what her naan called an "*ogichidaa*." A warrior. A big tree. And lightning was always attracted to big trees. Split asunder. That's what they all wanted to do to her mother. And that's exactly what they did. Split her asunder. With a muzzleloader.

Today made it exactly six years since she was shot outside a restaurant in neighboring Minocqua at 3:48 p.m. Her mother had gone there armed only with the conviction that her husband was having an affair (which he was) and that she desperately wanted out of their marriage.

Over the years Shawna has heard from a lot of people who were there that day. The stories were all mostly the same: there was a confrontation, her mother yelling, grabbing the other woman by her hair briefly before seeming to have a moment of clarity, whereupon she calmly told her husband that she was divorcing him, that he was free to carry on with his white-trash whore. And then her mother walked out into the parking lot.

From there on out it got a little blurry. Some said the two spoke in the parking lot, that her mother said something into his ear before walking to her car. Shawna had gone through a million possibilities of what her mother's final words might have been before her step-father reached into his truck and grabbed the rifle.

-You aren't a real man.

-I never loved you.

-My daughter has always hated you.

-You fuck like a donkey.

-Without your whiteness you are nothing.

-Your balls are filled with death.

-Go ahead. I will haunt you for the rest of your sad, empty life.

This last one gave Shawna the most comfort. Not that there was much comfort to be had when a man shot your mother through the front window of her car in broad daylight. The police said he might have been coming after Shawna next since when they eventually stopped him on his way back into Mercer, the rifle on the seat beside him had been reloaded. There were times Shawna wished he'd gotten to her. Times she wished she was wherever her mother was now. And her mother *was* somewhere. Shawna knew that much. And she knew that if it wasn't for her naan and Elmer, Shawna would be in that somewhere too.

Shawna took the helmet off, placed it on her lap. "Spidey powers," she said. "I wish I'd had them the day that fucker shot her."

"What are we doing here, Shawna?"

For an answer, Shawna nudged the duffle bag at her feet. In the moonlight, Douglas could see a bow, some arrows. Socks were balled up on the ends of the arrows, wire holding them to the broadheads. The plan had been to set fire to the house. Her step-dad's best friend. And also the closest thing to her actual step-dad since, unfortunately, he was safe in prison.

"Soaked them in lamp oil," Shawna said. "I was going to set his house on fire."

"Because he's friends with your step-dad?"

"Because he's evil."

Shawna could feel Douglas staring at her, could feel his concern, and something about it made her want to jump right out of the boat. He would never understand what it was like. Why had she brought him there anyway? He was white. Like Peyton. Like all of them cheese-and-Slim-Jim-eating bastards. Elmer. That's who should be with her. But she knew even Elmer would have tried to stop her. Nobody, whatever color, had the same thing growing inside them. Shawna felt her heart pounding, her hand tightening around nothing.

"C'mon," Douglas suddenly said, startling her. "You want to set something on fire? I know just the thing."

———————

A SPOT-LIGHT SAFEGUARDED the town Loon as they sat on a bench used by tourists. The duffle bag rested at Shawna's feet.

"I got my picture taken under this thing when I was a kid," Shawna said, staring up at the black beak looming over them.

"Me, too. Except my dad used to call this The Ugly White Duck. I thought that's what loons were called until, like, the third grade."

Shawna remembered what she'd said about his dad's spirit being trapped in the Loon. If that were somehow true, she wondered if what they were about to do might somehow help him on his way. "You know what the word Ojibwa means?"

"No."

"It means to *roast until puckered*. Something to do with how we used to make moccasins."

"Then I bet when we're finished, it'll look like a giant roasted marshmallow."

"C'mon," she said, picking up the duffle bag. "You'll need to light them. I think four ought to do it."

They positioned themselves with Douglas holding the lighter under the socks, the broadheads just pushing through the material. In seconds, they came to life dripping with flame.

"The bow is pretty low-poundage," Shawna told him. "So the flame won't go out when I release. I've been practicing."

Without another word, Shawna let the first one fly. It lofted and arched through the air before thunking into the Loon's breast. Two more found their way into the head and another, just for good measure, into the bird's crotch. It all happened faster than Shawna expected, the giant flames whooshing up, the fat white belly of the Loon quickly engulfed.

CHAPTER FIVE
Kay

KAY WOKE AT 3:23 a.m. in a cold sweat and shuffled into the living room, patting the urn on top of the TV as she passed. "How about a little tennis? No? Well, too bad. Change the channel if you don't like it."

Because they didn't have cable, she could only get the tennis matches early in the morning. It was one of the few perks of insomnia, though she rarely managed to stay awake all that long. This night was no different; hours later she woke in a field of bristling static. She'd been dreaming of him again. Norm giving their young son a bath back in their home in Michigan, the one Kay had never really wanted to move from. Her best friend Corky had been in the dream, too. They'd been sitting on the edge of a pool somewhere, legs dangling, the sound of children playing nearby. Corky never did have children. She had both pitied and envied that in her friend. Up until the very end, Corky had been strong, refusing, after the first round of chemo had failed, to return to the hospital no matter what her family might have wanted her to do. And she'd done it all without God. Even that, her *not*-believing, no matter how much it may have differed from Kay's own beliefs, impressed her.

Kay had been there for those last days. Corky had asked her to come, to "watch" as she put it. There were others there, of course, other family members, other friends, but there had always been a special connection between her and Corky. Like Corky had always been trying to teach Kay something, show her how life *could* be lived. And maybe that's why she wanted Kay to be there at the end, too. To show her how to die. To show her how death *could* be.

Kay made her way back to bed. From atop the dresser, Don Quixote stared down at her. Douglas must have placed the statue there recently; she hadn't seen the thing in years. She remembered how sometimes Norm would mention the statue when telling her about his day at the shop. *Somebody asked about Don again today. I told them he was a trophy I won at a jousting tournament. They thought I was serious. Doesn't anybody read anymore?* God, how she missed him. Even all his irritating habits. The way he'd groan when getting up and down from the sofa, something she now found herself starting to do. Even his god-awful snoring she missed. She'd gotten used to it at some point over the years, relied on it the way some people did the hum of a fan or those soothing CDs with whale sounds.

As she lay there looking up at the solemn wooden face, she found herself wondering what horses dreamt of. Galloping, probably. Through fields of apples and little girls in bonnets. Something like that. Or maybe being ridden into battle, their manes being gripped tight, nostrils flaring, muscles screaming with life. As for her own dreams, they kept Corky and Norm alive. And maybe they *were* alive, at least in the world of dreams. Maybe that was part of death. Maybe not everything was accounted for. The thought calmed her for some reason. "Take me into the trenches, Seven," she said to the blanket as she pulled it up under her chin. "Let's go."

SHE CRINGED WHEN she saw it was after eleven in the morning. What would Norm think if he could see her now? She glanced irritably up at the ceiling as she eased herself out of bed. "I know, I know," she muttered. "But it's not like anybody's waiting for me." Douglas had, no doubt, already come and gone by now. She shuffled to the bathroom and began brushing her teeth. "Not like I've got to cook you breakfast, is it? Not like Douglas needs lunch made." She spit into the sink. On the countertop, tucked under the round swivel-mirror Norm had used for shaving, was a book. *Animals Attack!* The old fool was always reading books about people surviving out in the wild or people being attacked by animals. The man could fashion a bear trap from twigs and a length of squirrel gut but figuring out how to put up a curtain rod in the front room had conveniently remained a mystery to him.

Kay picked the book up, opened it to a spot held by a faded, green sticky note. *While being drug off by the leopard, the bloody outer garment had fallen from the woman's body.* Kay closed the book, left it on the sink as a reminder to herself to remove it from the bathroom. "I never understood you or your fascination with these things," she said to the mirror as she combed her hair. "Such a dark mind you had. What were you thinking in there all those years?" Her hair was still mostly black. Lately, though, the silver had started weaving its way through. "A tough old bird," she said to the mirror and smirked. "A tough old bird who wakes up at noon. What do you think of that, Norm?"

After a breakfast of toast, Kay grabbed her walking stick and headed outside. Seven was there in his pen. When he heard her coming, his ears stiffened and began to twitch. Kay understood it to mean she should tread lightly, that he wasn't yet comfortable with her, so she sat in an old plastic lawn chair outside the gate that Shawna sometimes used.

"It's just me," she said more loudly than she intended to. "Not scared of a little old lady, are you?" He had to have been cold out there last night even with the thick blanket Shawna had him wear. It could get bad, dipping down into the forties sometimes. Kay shivered at the thought of it and snuggled into the oversized Carhartt she'd taken to wearing. It had been Norm's, the one he'd worn to the shop every day. It stank of grease and engine oil and cigarettes.

While she waited for the horse to settle down, Kay found herself staring at a clod of dandelions at her feet. There weren't many in the yard, at least not like when they'd lived in Michigan. She nudged the weeds with her foot. *Just this*, she thought. *If I could somehow grasp just this one thing, hold it and digest it fully and completely in my head, then I'd understand everything.* She'd been having these kinds of thoughts, these little side conversations with God, more and more frequently lately. A part of her wanted to dig up the weed and bring it inside to study, but she stopped herself before doing such a silly thing.

The horse snorted, wagging its head from side to side like it had water in its ears. "I'm already losing it, Seven. What do you say to that?" Kay peered out through the trees toward the lake. The water was choppy, the wind creating miniature waves that would push the foam further up the bank. Soon the foam would cover the entire lake, then slowly turn darker and darker shades of yellow until it looked something like ash, like a volcano in a nearby town had erupted. It surprised her every year how the ice crept like a living thing over the water come winter. She sat forward in the chair, the arms and legs twisting as she did. Such a durable thing and yet so flimsy. There was something to that, something significant maybe, but she couldn't quite put her finger on it.

Seven pawed at the ground, snorted. She couldn't imagine the animal sick, couldn't imagine him having something like a massive heart attack. Seven was pure life. It emanated from him. He was a spark. A spark waiting to turn into flame. Kay stood up slowly, took a step toward the animal. He was calmer, only stamping lightly at the ground now. She remembered something Douglas had told her one night while she had been drinking but hadn't been sure if she'd heard him right. *Shawna says that what we call a hoof is really just a toe. Apparently they used to have five toes but over time it evolved into just the one.* She remembered how the girl wanted to be a veterinarian one day. And she wished it for the girl. More than anything she wished it. But it wouldn't be easy. Nothing, really, would ever be easy for the girl. "So you had feet a long time ago?" she said quietly. "Well, not you, but your ancestors. What do you think about that? Would you like to have five toes? Probably make it hard to run. You'd constantly be getting rocks stuck in there."

Kay looked at the chair, then back at Seven again. She wanted to know what it felt like to be spark and flame. Or maybe what it felt like to be Don Quixote. Maybe she could use her walking stick to joust at the old ladies down at church, the ones who were always gobbling cookies and gossiping in the church basement. She took another step closer to the pen and Seven's gigantic head swung toward her, his nose bobbing up and down like he was agreeing with her every thought. She dug into her pocket, pulled out a handful of baby carrots she'd brought from home. "Don't eat me," she said, cautiously sliding her hand through the metal bars. "Just the carrots now, okay?"

Seven's head lowered and his lips and muzzle engulfed the carrots in one take. Kay took a step back, wondering what the equivalent in human food was that she'd just given him. Probably something like a tic-tac. Kay hugged Norm's coat tight against her and noticed some hay stacked against the garage. It looked like alfalfa, but Kay couldn't be sure. She hadn't really touched a bale of hay since she was a girl helping her uncle on his farm in Michigan. She remembered tagging along after him as he fed the goats and cows. Wasn't there a sow she'd taken to? It was all so fragmented now. What she wouldn't give to be transported back into her little girl body for just a few hours. She'd run and run across that farm and through the fields and just keep running until her time ran out.

She continued on her walk, inhaling and savoring as

she went. There was still magic in the air, though she had to breathe deep to taste it, and it hurt a little to do so. It was like the magic from her childhood was hanging there on the end of a long string, tethered like a brittle kite that was threatening to disintegrate if she tugged too hard at it. Just like an old memory, she mused as she moved down the road in something like a half-hobble.

When she got home over an hour later, she made herself a drink and nestled into Norm's old spot on the couch. She pressed the button on the remote a few times but nothing happened. "Christ, are you kidding me?" She aimed it again at the TV like a gun and pressed down harder on the red button. Nothing. She noticed a little silver screw on the back. She rocked herself back and forth, gaining momentum to propel herself upright. In the kitchen, she dug through the "crap drawer" with all the batteries and stamps and other miscellaneous things, and when she found two triple-As hiding in the back, she felt a tiny rush of accomplishment. Once she made it back to the couch and was comfortably settled in again, she realized she'd forgotten to grab a screwdriver. Something about this irritated her to no end, and, for a brief second, she could feel herself wanting to cry. The frustration was there behind her eyes, the squeeze of it coursing through her whole body and wanting out. She took a deep breath. *You're okay,* she told herself and reached for her drink.

All the screwdrivers they had were too big, so Kay dug through Norm's top dresser drawer where he kept all his knick-knacks. She knew he had a Gerber somewhere that might work, but while looking for it she came across an old blue bag with a yellow drawstring. *Seagram's Crown*

Royal. At one time, she knew he'd kept his poker chips in it, but opening it now she found a few old matchbooks and a silver key. Kay put the key in her coat pocket and dug out one of the matchbooks. *Les Deux Magots, 6 Place Saint-Germain-des-Prés, 75006 Paris, France.* There was a picture on the front of a woman sitting outside a café drinking coffee. She wore a yellow dress with a matching yellow bonnet, the kind with a veil that used to be popular in France back in the forties. She knew Norm had once been on leave in France, had spent time in Paris, but he'd never spoken about it much. And, as far as she knew, had nothing but contempt for the French. Or "frogs" as he always called them.

She found the Gerber behind an old pack of playing cards and turned it over in her hand, feeling the heft of it. She'd seen Norm open the thing countless times but had never paid all that much attention. *Didn't he squeeze it? Yes, he squeezed it and it popped open.* She tried this, but nothing happened. Her hands were shaking now. She wasn't okay. *This* wasn't okay. Why couldn't he be there to help her? She squeezed again to the point where she was afraid she'd break the dumb thing. Her hands wouldn't stop trembling. There was a hotness behind her eyes, too, an anger mixing with the tears that were now starting to fall. She was afraid she wouldn't be able to stop if she gave into it. She went back into the living room and sat on the couch and squeezed harder and harder, putting all the hotness into her hand, but the tears kept dropping one by one, and suddenly it was all too much, the Gerber, the slow vanishing that would soon consume her, the afternoon and the light it was holding outside the window, and she threw the remote across the room, threw it as hard as she could without looking where she was throwing it because the world was blurry now, and she heard it crash against the wall, or maybe the TV, she didn't care which, and when she looked up and wiped her face with her sleeve she realized it wasn't the TV, or the wall, but the urn on top of the TV that the remote had hit. At first, she was worried that the ashes might have spilled out, but they hadn't. Only the top had come off, the bag lying there intact on the carpet and through the tears she started to laugh, a heaving sob of a laugh that erupted in big chunks she couldn't control. *Pike shit.* She had thought about dumping the ashes in the lake once, the way other people do in the ocean or off a mountain top, but somehow that didn't seem right either since Norm always said the lake was mostly full of seaweed and pike shit. She eased herself off the couch and crawled on her hands and knees over to the urn and carefully placed the ashes back where they belonged. She wasn't laughing now. Or crying.

She felt rested.

Like she'd just woken from a long nap.

CHAPTER SIX
Douglas

THE SUN WAS setting behind the Wampum Shop as Douglas went about picking up the oil rags Marty had once again left scattered just about everywhere. Marty was busy at the computer, busy pretending he wasn't looking at fish porn.

"You almost done over there?"

"Huh? Oh, yeah, I finished like ten minutes ago."

Douglas shook his head, tossed the handful of dirty rags into the bin by the back door. It had been busier than usual that day for some reason, people coming in for oil changes and alignments one after the other. Marty actually had to earn his pay that day, which meant cutting down on the socializing. And even though Marty's talent for small talk usually annoyed Douglas no end, he also knew that it kept him in business, that it provided his customers with something he himself wasn't very good at.

"You wanna grab a beer?" Douglas asked once they'd gotten the shop all squared away. "My treat."

"Naw," Marty said. "I better head home."

"Since when do you pass up free beer? Scratch that. Since when do you pass up free anything?"

Marty shrugged but didn't say anything. There was no comeback, no return insult, which worried Douglas a little. He'd been acting strange lately, and, for a while, Douglas attributed this to Norm's death. But now he wasn't so sure. "So I'm the one who did it. Well, Shawna and I did."

"Did what?"

"Burnt down the loon."

"Fuck off you did."

Douglas smiled to himself but didn't say anything more.

"I'm shocked. What did that bird ever do to you?"

"Shawna needed to let off some steam, and I guess I thought the loon seemed like a safe option."

Marty shook his head. "So much for liberal guilt."

"I thought you'd be proud of me."

"For what? Turning pyro?"

"I don't know. Just don't go telling anyone, okay?"

"Yeah, we'll see."

"Marty..."

"Okay, fine. I won't tell anyone."

"Hey, I've been meaning to ask you something. Shawna seems to think you were at one of those fishing rights protests. Is that true?"

Marty seemed caught off guard by the question, fumbling with his keys before finally answering. "I only went once. It was stupid. I left when people started throwing shit."

"So you weren't yelling things at people?"

Marty shook his head. "I might be an asshole, but I'm not that breed of asshole."

When Marty got in his truck, Douglas walked over, said, "So are you doing okay? You seem a little off. Well, more off than usual."

Marty stuck the keys in the ignition. "It's nothing for you to worry your pretty little head about." For a few seconds, Marty played with the keys dangling in the ignition like maybe he was going to say something more but, instead, just smiled weakly and started the engine. Douglas kept quiet, waved once he drove off. He knew from experience Marty wasn't about to tell him about anything until he was good and ready.

Douglas was debating whether to go solo to the tavern or go home and check in on his mom when he noticed someone walking towards the shop. The figure was silhouetted against the backdrop of the road and the setting sun, afire with pinks and purples.

"My knight in shining armor," the figure said.

The halo of fire, Douglas soon realized, was due more to the redness of the person's hair than the departing sun. "Jenna?" he said quietly, a hand shielding his eyes as if he'd blind himself should he look at her directly.

"The one and lonely."

Douglas had a hard time imagining somebody like Jenna being lonely, but he nodded anyway. "Headed home?"

"I was," she said, coming to a stop. There was a slight chill to the air now, and her breath came out in white puffs. "But my car decided it was going on strike. No advance warning or anything. Can you believe that?"

"The nerve," Douglas said, seeing where this was going. "You want me to take a look?"

"Looks like you were just leaving for the day, weren't you? I'm really sorry. I wouldn't ask, but it's not like I can call a taxi out here, can I?"

"You could, but it would take Morris about an hour to get here. And there's no guarantee he'd show up sober."

"I'll make you the best cup of coffee you've ever tasted..."

"That wouldn't be too hard to do," Douglas said, putting his car keys back in his pocket. "Dad always kept Maxwell House at the shop if that tells you anything."

Douglas walked with her, his tool bag slung over his shoulder, and during the short walk they talked about her painting, how running the shop was taking up more of her time than she had expected. "But I guess I don't have to tell you about that, do I?"

Douglas wanted to tell her how running the shop was fairly new to him, but he knew that doing so would open up a whole different conversation he wasn't, for once, quite in the mood for. At least not with her. Not yet. "Have you thought about painting at the shop? I mean, behind the counter or something when you have breaks."

"Breaks? What are those?"

"Is it that busy?"

She pulled her hair back as she walked, twisting it into a sort of braid and then releasing it again. It revealed her neck for just a split second, the path of small hairs there.

"It gets busy enough sometimes," she said, "but it's all the prep and cleaning and ordering that's really keeping me busy. I think if I set an easel up behind the counter all it would do is remind me that I'm not painting, you know?"

Douglas nodded. Drawing, for him, was a luxury now. Something he often missed while at work. And sometimes in the evening, when his hands were cramped from, say, being wrapped around a lug wrench all day, the simple act of drawing seemed monumental.

"How about you?" she asked after a bit. "You drawing much?"

"On and off, I guess. It's not something I keep track of."

She looked at him hard, like she was listening to a song on the radio she couldn't quite make out the lyrics to. He could tell she wanted to ask him something more, but, for whatever reason, she kept quiet.

Once they got to the coffee shop, Jenna handed him her car keys and went inside to make him something. He was already pretty certain what the problem was based on what she'd told him so far, but he went ahead and put the key in and tried to turn it over anyway. Nothing. He jiggled the gear shift a little and tried again, but the trick didn't work, so he popped the hood. At times like these, he felt like a dentist. Rooting around, looking for things that maybe weren't a problem yet but soon would be if not taken care of. By the time he'd finished the examination, he counted two other cavities besides the one rotten-tooth starter. Deciding to keep quiet about the worn serpentine belt, he leaned back against the front fender and watched Jenna inside the shop. She'd turned on all the lights and it felt a little like he was watching a fish in a fish tank. There was something about the way she moved, almost like she was lighter than other people, like she wasn't tethered to the same mundane things. He didn't stand a chance with her. He knew that much. She was just in need of a little help and he reminded himself not to start thinking it was anything more than that. Besides, even if there were some interest on her part, it would soon be gone once she'd gotten a look at his drawings.

"What's the verdict?" she said as she came out with a steaming cup in her hands. "Benign or malignant? Give it to me straight."

Douglas couldn't remember which of those were worse, so he just took the cup and said thank you.

"It's probably still a little hot. You might want to give it a second or two."

Douglas nodded and thought about how best to explain things. He didn't want to come off like the guy at the electronics store in Minocqua who kept rattling off strange words Douglas didn't understand when trying to explain why the repair shop's computer was fried. There was contempt there, of Douglas's ignorance of all things computer-related. It was similar to how the doctor had seemed to be annoyed when describing what had happened to his dad.

...acute myocardial infarction...bitmap...congestive heart failure...recursive function...coronary thrombosis... terabytes...

"It's probably your solen--" Douglas started to say, but then caught himself. "It's probably your starter, but I'll need to get under the car to check. Do you know if you have a jack?"

Jenna looked at the engine as he talked, nodding her head like she knew just what he was talking about. It was something most of his customers did, something Douglas himself did when talking to the computer guy and doctor even though he'd been completely lost in both cases.

"I think there's one in the trunk," Jenna said, but when Douglas started walking around behind the car, she stopped him. "Do we really need to worry about this? I mean, it's not like you'll be able to fix it right now anyway, right?"

"No, I guess not. I'd have to order you one."

"Well then," she said, "I guess it'll have to keep until tomorrow."

"I was thinking of going to the bar. Would you maybe want to--"

"I don't drink."

"Oh," Douglas said, picturing the empty bottles sitting on the kitchen counter back home. "Sorry. I didn't know."

"It's a long, boring story. I'll tell you about it sometime if you want."

"Yeah. Okay."

"Take a sip."

"What?"

"Of your coffee. You haven't tried it yet."

"Oh. Right."

Douglas did as he was told and swallowed what tasted like a blowtorch dipped in chocolate. "Whoa," he said, his tongue melting. "You sure this doesn't have alcohol in it?"

"Just some flavored coffee. And a sprinkle of magic maybe."

"Well, whatever it is, it's good."

"Maybe I should open up a coffee shop."

"I wouldn't go that far."

Douglas offered to get his car and return to give her a ride home, but she insisted on walking back with him after she'd locked up. There weren't many cars out, but, as they neared the repair shop, one slowed, and a man leaned out the window. "Your girlfriend's a whore!" Douglas noted the license plates. *Illinois.* He was about to apologize to Jenna when he saw that she had her middle finger raised high in the air. And she was smiling. The bastard in the car must have seen this because he stopped right there in the middle of the road, the red of his tail lights reflecting off the pavement.

"They're not from here," Douglas pointed out. "They're probably just drunk."

"They're probably just assholes," Jenna said, lowering her hand.

He expected an argument from her, but Jenna kept quiet as he approached the idling car. Douglas found himself thinking, once again, of his father. He could almost see him slapping the roof of the car, asking, in a tone that was somehow both friendly and intimidating, if they were lost and needed any help. But that wasn't Douglas. He wasn't his father. Not even close.

As it turned out, though, there wasn't much of anything for Douglas to handle. Just as he was coming up on the car, it started to slowly creep forward. He could hear something being smashed inside the car, then a crumpled-up beer can being tossed from the driver's side. Once the car picked up speed and disappeared down the road, Douglas picked up the empty.

"And that's why I don't drink," Jenna said. "What a bunch of creeps."

"I'm sorry about that. They aren't from here," he said again stupidly. "Not that that helps any."

"It doesn't." She grabbed his hand, squeezing it, like she were the one comforting him. "Thank you, though," she said. "For trying."

Once they got his car, Douglas drove them out onto highway 51 and then down county road FF. Jenna's house was much the same as his parents': a green tin roof and a cluttered backyard that led down to a lake. The only thing different on the outside, as far as Douglas could tell, was the siding. There was none.

"I'm having it replaced. Demo'd it myself, though. To save money."

"Winter will be here soon."

"It'll get done."

Douglas didn't say anything but depending on who she

called to do the work, chances were it *wouldn't* get done. People didn't hurry much in Mercer. It was something he figured grew up out of the gray solitude of the place. In a way, it was very European. There was never much hurry. About anything. And the sooner she came to understand that, the sooner she'd find peace in Mercer.

"Will you come in for a few minutes?" she asked as she got out. "I wanted to show you something."

When Jenna opened the screen door, it creaked just like theirs at home. Douglas followed her inside, half-expecting to see his mom snoring on the couch, her mouth hanging open, the TV hissing white. But, instead, Douglas found a dog wagging its tail.

"Douglas, meet Shredder. Shredder, this is Douglas. He's going to visit for a little bit."

Douglas knelt down in front of the dog and let it lick his face.

"He likes you."

Jenna opened the door and let the dog out. Douglas wondered if she was aware of the wolves in the area, if the dog knew to stay near the house or not. It was a big dog, some sort of brown lab mix. A tennis-ball chaser. And maybe a deer chaser if he was unlucky enough to come across any. Douglas had once seen a neighbor's dog, an old weather-beaten Siberian husky, being chased down the street by a deer with its rack lowered like a snow plow.

"This is what I wanted to show you," Jenna said, walking over to an easel and turning it around. "It's still a work in progress, so, you know, keep that in mind."

It was similar in size to the others hanging in her

shop, only slightly more subdued in subject matter. In the painting was a wheelchair with a baby sitting in it. There was a food tray connected to the wheelchair, and, on the tray, a marriage certificate alongside a photo of a young smiling couple. The overall effect was somehow both creepy and beautiful. Which, now that Douglas thought about it, was exactly how he'd felt when he'd first seen the paintings in her shop.

"I don't know if I get it," Douglas said, feeling Jenna hovering behind him. "But I like it."

"You don't think it's too macabre?"

"A little, maybe. But is that a bad thing?"

"No, I guess not. And Shredder seems to like this one for some reason. When I was working on it, he'd just sit on the couch and wag his tail. It was a little weird."

They heard a scratching at the door and Jenna let the dog in. Douglas went back to looking at the painting, at the expression on the baby's face. The face was wizened, almost like an old man's. It was the focal point of the painting, the place your eyes kept going back to.

"Can I ask you something? About the painting, I mean."

"You want to know what it means."

"Or is it not supposed to matter? I've heard that from some artists." He paused a little, suddenly feeling ridiculous. "Okay, so I read that somewhere. I guess I've never actually talked to any real artists."

Jenna turned the painting so that it faced the couch and

took a seat. When Douglas didn't follow suit, she patted the cushion next to her.

"I guess it's sort of like a memoir." She paused, staring at the painting. "Can I see something of yours sometime? I promise not to judge."

"Sure," Douglas said, "but prepare yourself for massive disappointment."

Jenna ignored this artfully by sipping from her coffee and simply arching an eyebrow at him before telling him her story.

"I was married once. To a wonderful man. But then, one day, everything changed when he was hurt at work." She paused and looked at Douglas. "I'm sorry, I better start earlier. I don't talk much about this, so it's not so easy for me."

"However is fine," Douglas said. "Or not at all, if you don't want to."

"No, I want to. It's good for me. At least that's what they say."

My dad died.

"Okay," she said, her eyes settling on the painting again. "So Matt used to paint bridges. We were young and had met in college and both of us wanted to be artists. After we graduated, he took this job painting bridges because he liked to be outside and both of us wanted to travel. So he takes this job and soon we're moving across the country from one city to another, usually only staying for a few months at a time. This went on for a couple of years. Both of us were pretty happy. I didn't have to work because we didn't need much. I was painting like crazy then. Just staying home most days, or maybe going for a walk if I felt like it. What I'm trying to say, Douglas, is that I was happy. It wasn't perfect, of course. We still had our quarrels. But, overall, looking back, I was the definition of ignorant bliss." She stopped again. Douglas figured she was probably trying to compose herself. He had noticed a slight quiver come into her voice, something trying to shake loose, but when she started speaking again it was gone. "Then he fell and broke his back. The doctors said he was lucky to be alive, but, and I know this is going to sound shitty, it never felt all that lucky. What I mean is that the Matt I brought home from the hospital that day wasn't the same Matt I married. That fall broke more than his back. He turned, changed into something, someone, I didn't recognize. I tried, Douglas. I really did. I did everything for him. Changed him, bathed him, fed him, wiped him. You name it, I did it. And I did it with kindness. I truly did. But that didn't seem to matter. Nothing did. He became angry. Hateful and bitter." Again, she paused, looking at the floor now. "Have you ever seen an abused animal? You know, the ones they find half-starved and beaten in a basement somewhere? You have to be careful if you try to help them because they'll try to bite you. That's how it was with Matt. No matter what I did, he'd snarl and try to tear my throat out. I stayed with it, though, for about two years. Which may not sound like a long time to you, but, trust me, it was. I had no life of my own. Everything I did, I did for Matt. Every second of my day belonged to him in some way."

"That's why the baby."

"That's why the baby. You must think I'm horrible."

"I don't think that."

"Well, I do. Or, I used to. Anyway, one day I'd had enough. He'd called me a talentless whore one too many times, and I just up and left. I called his mother, who never liked me much to begin with, and told her I was done. I left with nothing, took nothing except my clothes. Can you try to remember that when I tell you what I did next?"

"Okay."

"We were living in Oregon at that time. To be close to his parents. Which is where he's still living now, I think."

"You haven't spoken to him?"

"Not in five years. When he told me he'd signed the divorce papers, he started crying, telling me he'd changed, that he was sorry for how he treated me. But it was too late by then. I wasn't the same person anymore."

"But how'd you end up here? I mean, you could have gone anywhere. Mercer's not exactly a bucket-list destination."

"I didn't actually go anywhere for about a year. But he didn't know that. I told him and his family that I was moving back to San Diego. That's where most of my family is."

"But you stayed?"

"I stayed. And because I needed money, I started dancing."

Douglas was about to ask what kind of dancing she did, but then he realized what she meant. They had dancers there, too, up in Hurley. He'd gone once. The girl was nice, kept talking to him and Marty while she swung drunkenly around the pole. It hadn't been anything like what Douglas had expected. The talking part had made him feel like he was at a barber shop.

"You started stripping."

"Yes. And drinking."

Douglas looked at the painting again. It wasn't a toy lying on the ground, or a streamer. It was a tassel.

"Does that bother you?"

"No," Douglas muttered. "Why would it?"

"Matt had been accusing me of sleeping around for as long as I could remember, so I guess I sort of saw it as a kind of self-fulfilling prophecy. Not that I was actually sleeping with the customers, but you know what I mean."

Douglas nodded. She went on to tell him that at first it had terrified her, getting up on stage in front of strange men, that she'd never been very confident before, or even that much of a dancer really, but that after a while she started to get better at it. And, eventually, even came to like it.

"I made friends there. Good friends. It was like a whole new family." She smiled at him, stroked Shredder's head which was now resting on her lap, a ringlet of drool seeping into her jeans. "I miss them. They've all promised to visit me here someday, but I doubt it'll ever happen. Mercer wouldn't know how to handle them."

"No," Douglas said. "Probably not."

They were quiet for a bit, both of them staring down at Shredder, when, in a near-whisper, Jenna said, "Do you think you know how to handle me?"

It startled Douglas at first. Her voice was different. Lower. Thicker. Almost like he could taste it.

"I could try."

Jenna smiled and nudged Shredder off her lap. Then she stood up and turned the painting around so that it was facing the wall again. "C'mon then," she said, holding her hand out to him. "Prove it."

CHAPTER SEVEN
Shawna

THE LAKE OF the Torches Casino was busy Saturday night. Shawna clocked out for her break a few minutes early so she wouldn't be late meeting up with Elmer out on the receiving dock. He always took his breaks there so he could smoke in private. And while Shawna didn't smoke, she often found that sitting with him calmed her.

"Hey," she said, pulling up a crate. She counted two butts on the ground already obliterated by Elmer's shoe.

Elmer nodded, took a drag of his American Spirit. Shawna had always thought it funny that he smoked the brand. It was a white person thing to do.

"How are you?" he asked quietly after a bit.

"I'm okay. Just another magical night in busser heaven."

He smiled a little, nodded toward the fence a ways in front of them. "Could be worse."

Beyond the fence was a row of ramshackle houses and

a shirtless little boy chasing his dog with a stick. She could see somebody wearing a robe sitting in a chair, a hand with a beer rising and falling every few seconds, the faint din of a TV going that nobody was watching.

"I'm sorry about the other night," Elmer said quietly. "You know. On the island."

"Not your fault," Shawna said back just as softly.

"There's a noose around that kid's neck and he doesn't even know it."

Shawna kept quiet, watching the boy and the dog. There was no telling what waited for the boy inside that house later, no telling how long that hand had been rising and falling.

"Why do you smoke those?"

Elmer turned and looked at her. His hair fell over his plump cheeks, cheeks that seemed to her almost like a baby's. "I used to smoke them Camels, but they're not as good."

Shawna reached out, tucked some of his hair behind his ear. Elmer Rising Sun rolled his eyes at her. She knew he was seeing himself running around that backyard while his mother drank on the porch. Shawna was about to tell him about burning the loon down with Douglas, something she'd been putting off because she was afraid he'd get jealous, when she heard somebody whistle nearby.

"Hey, this where we go to file a complaint?"

Shawna immediately stood up when she saw the three men, but Elmer remained sitting, staring off at the little boy. It was almost like he'd been expecting them.

"You people get a kick out of this, don't you, watching all us white people throw away our hard-earned pay? Well, we don't think it's so funny. My buddy here lost over a thousand dollars. Now what's he supposed to tell his wife when he goes home?"

The faces of the men were all pasty-looking and puffy, like they'd been up all night drinking. The smallest one, the one doing the talking, seemed to be the leader. Shawna, in a voice as solid as she could manage, said, "Maybe you should tell her you suck at gambling."

There was silence for a few seconds, the two big ones swaying there, dumbfounded, before the little one spoke again. "Hey, that's pretty good. What's your name, sweetheart?"

"Go home."

"Well, now, that's a funny name. Isn't that a funny name, Marcus?"

Marcus, the one who'd lost the money, looked like he was about to lunge at Shawna. "I bet her real name is Squaw Bitch."

Elmer slowly stood up, like he'd only just noticed them. "Tell me," he said, "where do *we* go to file a complaint?"

"A complaint for what?" the ringleader said. "You lose some scalps or something?"

The others laughed at this. One of them even puckered his lips and began bouncing the palm of his hand off his mouth.

"We lost our land and our people," Elmer said, hopping

down from the dock. "Now you tell me where we go to get a refund for that."

The little one began to snigger and Shawna jumped down, went to stand by Elmer's side. If something were to happen, she decided she would fight right alongside Elmer. *Please,* she found herself thinking, *just try something.* One of the men started to lumber toward them, but the little one held him back. "No," he told him, his voice a hiss, "not here." The big one nodded his head, reluctantly backed off.

"Okay, chief," the leader said to Elmer, turning and walking back the way they'd come. "We'll be back. You can bet on that."

Elmer and Shawna both stayed quiet, watching. Shawna placed her hand in Elmer's as they left, her anger soon swallowed up by his calm. Something that happened, she realized, more often than she'd care to admit.

"We should get drunk," Shawna said after a bit, "and show up at their work some time."

"And vomit in the suggestion box."

"I bet they all work at an insurance company or a bank or something."

"And they beat their wives."

"With bibles."

As they headed back inside to finish their shifts, Shawna looked back and saw the little boy standing at the fence. His face was blank. It was an expression she'd seen many times on her people. One of being lost. Of disbelief rather than wonder. She could almost feel the sick in the pit of the boy's stomach. She waved to him and the boy waved back, the expression on his face not changing one bit. Behind him, the hand on the porch went up and back down again. The dog barked. And then Shawna went back inside to scrape potatoes and half-eaten eggs from the plates of strangers.

THE REST OF the night moved at a slower pace than usual, and by the time Shawna's shift was over all she wanted to do was go home and crawl into bed. Her body ached and her feet throbbed from zigzagging among the tables all night. She tried to imagine herself married to Elmer, tried to picture him rubbing her feet when she got home and the two of them curling up on the couch to watch a movie. She tried, but she couldn't quite picture him that way. And it wasn't because he wouldn't rub her feet. She knew he would if she ever asked him to. It was something else. Almost like future-Shawna didn't exist.

Shawna found present-Elmer sitting on the hood of her car in the parking lot. He did this sometimes, usually because he wanted a ride home. Or the other. She hoped it wasn't the other. She was too tired tonight. Then again, Elmer always seemed to have this knack for giving her a second wind. She wasn't sure how he did it because, frankly, he wasn't all that charismatic. There were other boys far more interesting, far better looking, than Elmer. And she wouldn't have all that much trouble finding someone to keep her company seeing as most boys weren't all that complicated. They thought they were, but they weren't. Elmer was different, though. Even though four out of seven days a week he wore the same stupid *Slayer* t-shirt, even though he smoked too much, Shawna loved him. Because underneath all of that, Shawna saw the sadness. It was there when she was alone with him, when he kissed her. There was pain inside of him, rivers and rivers of it, similar to the ones that had been coursing through her ever since her mom died. And that was something other boys couldn't understand.

"Heya," she said. "You need a ride?"

He slid off the hood, tossing the cigarette down. "Sure."

"You don't say "sure," Elmer. You ask if that's okay, if I wouldn't mind."

"Would you mind?"

"C'mon, idiot," she said, opening the door for him. "Where to?"

"Don't matter," he said, sullen as a toddler.

"Fine. To a foot spa then."

As they waited at a stoplight in town, Shawna found herself staring at a fire hydrant. It resembled a little girl in a red coat, and, for some reason, this little girl looked to Shawna like she was about to jump off the sidewalk into traffic. When they got close to Elmer's, Shawna parked next to a basketball court about a block away from his place and cut the engine.

As Elmer waved at the smoke curling back into the car, Shawna found herself thinking about the fire hydrant again. Things like that had been happening to her more and more lately. It wasn't so much that she really thought she saw a little girl in a red coat standing on the corner instead of a fire hydrant. It was that a fear had come over her, a desperate urge to slam on the brakes and run out and save the girl. Even though it only lasted a few seconds, it had felt very real to her.

Elmer let out a long sigh and rested his hand on her thigh. It was awkward, the way he placed it there while looking out the open window. Like they were on a first date, rather than already having left scratches and bite marks on each other. She put her hand on top of his and then waited. It had become a sort of game to her, seeing how long Elmer could stand for her to touch him. Soon he'd reach for another cigarette, not because he wanted one, but because it would give him an excuse to pull his hand away. It was, she'd realized long ago, just how he was.

"You worried about school?" Shawna said, placing her hand on the steering wheel when Elmer pulled his away.

"A little, I guess."

He let out another long, heavy sigh and slid down the seat so that his head was resting on Shawna's lap. It was another rarity. And one Shawna didn't want to disturb. So, rather than do something as stupid as run her fingers through his hair, Shawna craned her head under the windshield to get a better look at the moon as it came out from behind a cluster of clouds. It wasn't a full moon, but it was close. The Freezing Moon. That's what her mother had called it. The moon that came after the Falling Leaves Moon.

"Do you remember the story of Chakabesh?" Shawna asked him.

"Sure. That's what my naan called me when I was a kid. I don't think she meant it affectionately, though."

"Do you remember the story?"

"Some."

"He never listened to his older sister."

"Yeah."

"She was always trying to warn him."

"But he would go off with his bow and arrow anyway."

"And he killed the elephant and inside he found the hair of his mother and father and he wanted to bring them back to life."

"But he didn't because death was natural or something? I can't remember."

"All I know is he didn't bring them back to life."

"No."

"I wouldn't either."

"Wouldn't what?"

"Bring my mother back to life." Another smaller group of clouds, darker and denser, passed over the moon and Shawna sat back.

"Sometimes I feel like the older sister," Elmer said, grinning at her. "Always trying to warn you about things."

"And I never listen." Shawna tugged at his t-shirt, pulling it up over his stomach, and ran her fingers along the thin hairs there. His stomach trembled a little, jumping under her touch. Shawna leaned down to kiss him, but just as she was about to close her eyes, she felt Elmer jerk back.

"Shawna..."

She looked up and there, peering in through the passenger side window, were three grotesque masks. Or, at least, that's what they first seemed like to Shawna, like those Halloween masks kids buy with those wide, creepy cut-out smiles that go all the way up to the ears. Only these were real human beings.

"Oh fuck oh fuck oh fuck." The words came out in a rush, running into one another as Shawna eased herself upright. Then one of the men outside made a roll-down-your-window gesture to Elmer.

"Don't," Shawna said, grabbing his arm. "We can just drive away."

"Just stay calm. I'll take care of it."

"You'll take care of all three of them?"

"If I have to."

Shawna let go of him. It was too late. It was in his voice. There was a turning in it. Something that had changed color. Elmer rolled his window down part way, and Shawna could smell the sourness of alcohol almost immediately as the puffy pink faces swayed there out in the dark.

"This a better time to talk, Tonto? Or maybe you want to finish up with your little squaw first?"

Shawna could see Elmer's hand reach for the door handle. "Don't," she pleaded again, hating how weak her voice sounded.

"It's okay, Cochise, you can come out. We won't hurt you. That wouldn't be fair, would it? Three against one." The small one leaned down and put his nose right up against the glass. He winked at Shawna. "What's a matter? You don't trust us?"

Shawna felt the weakness giving way to something else now. She leaned across Elmer, her words coming out like a growl. "Wannabe Custer motherfucker."

The other two men began to whistle and snicker at this, which made the little one bristle. "Your whore's got a mouth on her." This seemed to appease the other two as they stopped laughing. "You see," the little one went on, "we want our money back. You get me, Tonto? You do speak English, right? I always wondered about that. Why speak our language if you hate us so damn much? Why not going around speaking Featherhead or whatever it is you people speak?"

When Elmer just stared at them, the three men stepped back from the car and started whispering among themselves. After a minute or so, the little man bent down in front of Elmer's window again, and, with his voice barely above a whisper, said, "Last chance. How about you get out of the car like a good boy, and then I show your sister there how it's really done?"

"Gookoosh," Elmer muttered, and the little man cocked his head dramatically like he was trying hard to hear him.

"What's that? Hey, Carl. Big Red here said something in bushnigger." The little man peered back into the car. "Say it again, Red. C'mon now. What was it? Glucose or something? What's that mean? I bet it isn't very nice."

Shawna knew the word to mean "pig" in Ojibwa, and that was exactly what they looked like to her. Three drunk, angry pigs. And now one of them was behind the car. She wanted to run over as many of them as possible before driving out of there, but something was stopping her. Anger was stopping her. She didn't want to run. Her mother's voice rang out in her ears as clear as gunshot: *You will know the face of ignorance.* And suddenly it dawned on Shawna what her mother had been trying to tell her. "My phone," she muttered and started feeling around on the seat for it. "Have you seen my phone?"

"Shit, they're lying on the ground now," Elmer said, his hand still on the door handle. "One in front, one behind."

At first Shawna didn't understand what he was talking about, but then it clicked.

"If you want to leave, you'll have to kill one of them," the little one at the window said. "Or, and this is just a suggestion, you could get out and discuss this like a man."

Shawna turned on the dome light and spotted her phone on the floor by Elmer's feet.

"You should call Bill," he said, handing her the phone.

Bill Songetay was the tribal sheriff. She remembered once tossing a cigarette out her window, back when she smoked in high school, and Bill pulling her over, giving her the choice of getting a ticket for littering or picking up ten pieces of garbage along the roadside. And even though she had been annoyed at the time, she never threw anything out her window again.

"No, I'm going to record them."

Elmer looked at her. "Kind of dark for that, isn't it?"

Shawna fidgeted with the phone until she found the

right thing to tap and then handed it to Elmer, but the man had gone back to his car for something. "Here, point it in his face when he gets back."

Elmer craned his neck under the windshield and nodded toward the basketball court. "There're cameras up there, too, you know. From when all those fights kept breaking out."

Even though Shawna had moved off the reservation long ago when her mother had first gotten remarried, she remembered the cameras being a big deal when they'd first been put up. Many in the tribe saw it as a violation of their privacy. And some saw it as a white man's solution to their problems. And nobody much wanted that.

"Just try it. It might spook them."

"They aren't going to spook, Shawna. They're too drunk for that. I say we just run the assholes over."

"And have *that* on camera?"

"Oh, right."

Before Shawna could do much of anything, the little man sauntered back over with a six-pack dangling from his fingers and handed one to each of his buddies. Shawna and Elmer both noted the brand: Treaty Beer.

"You two ever tried this stuff? It's not half-bad. What's that line from that movie? *Tastes like...victory.*"

Shawna nudged Elmer, and he fumbled with the phone before holding it up to the window. "Whatcha got there? Hey, fellas, they're filming me! I'm gonna be an internet sensation!"

"Make sure to smile real purty!"

The voice came from behind them. Shawna could see the back of his bald head resting against the trunk of her car. She turned the engine over, gassed it. Both the men gave a start, crouching just in case they'd have to run. "Go slow," Elmer said, keeping the camera in the man's face. "They'll move."

Shawna revved it again and when she began inching forward, the one in front turned and placed his hands on the hood, bracing his feet in the gravel like maybe he thought he was Superman. Shawna let the car push forward. She could hear his feet skidding now, see the look on his face turn from leery bemusement to fear. The small one, seeing that his prey were escaping, began to punch at the window.

"That's it," Elmer teased him, smiling behind the phone, "keep swinging, little gookoosh."

Shawna had, until now, entirely forgotten about the horn. She expected it to do very little, but when she laid into it, the man in front jumped back like he'd been electrocuted. She gave it more gas, turning the wheel hard as she did, making sure there was a wide enough berth between her car and the drunks. Shawna was just starting to feel good, like they were in the clear, when she heard Elmer scream. It was a frightening sound, something between a bleating cow and a screaming child.

"Mmmmrrraaaaaaaarrrrrrggghhh!"

The little man had somehow managed to get his hand through the open window and was now hanging on to Elmer's ear. Shawna slammed on the brakes, but, just as she did, Elmer, who had both his hands around the man's thin arm, sank his teeth into him. There was another loud

CHAPTER EIGHT
Kay

IT WAS A Sunday, which meant it was count-the-do-nation- money day at church. Kay sat at an old card table in the basement un-crumpling dollar bills and working them into an envelope. Across from her sat Alma, a widow like herself, and someone Kay had only recently taken to calling a friend. She was often quiet, introspective it seemed to Kay, which made her different from the other blue-hairs, the gang of widows, who volunteered at the church and whose every word seemed to spring from some deep well of fear and loneliness. As if the act of talking signified life itself. As if even a moment's silence meant death was descending upon them. They always made Kay anxious.

"With all this money," Alma said quietly, conspirato-rially, "you'd think they could afford better coffee."

Kay shrugged. All coffee tasted pretty much the same to her. Like a cupful of dust. God knew she drank enough of it anyway, though. "With all this money, you'd think they could afford a better priest."

"Kay…"

"Well? You can't tell me it hasn't crossed your mind."

"I like him just fine."

"He wears sandals."

"He's hip. And they're called Birkenstocks. My Caroline has a pair."

"I don't want to see my priest's toes, thank you."

Alma laughed a little at this and shook out another pile of bills and coins onto the table. "I think he has nice feet."

"I don't care if they're nice or not; I don't want to see them. And did you know where he was before he came here? San Francisco. On *vacation*. What kind of priest goes to San Francisco on vacation?"

"A fun one?"

"A gay one. C'mon now. You know it as much as I do."

"I don't know that. I thought my Caroline's new boyfriend was gay, but she says he's definitely not and that just because he has a ponytail wrapped up into a ball on top of his head like a little pile of poo and does yoga and drinks white wine doesn't make him one."

"In Mercer it does."

"Well, maybe that's why they moved to Madison then."

At the table next to them, one of the blue hairs was giggling, tittering, over something one of the others had said. She sounded just like a little girl to Kay. Like a stupid, inexperienced little girl who had lived a sheltered life.

Everything was funny to them, always a smile on their faces. It made Kay's skin crawl. Because what they were laughing at was never actually all that funny.

"Father Jason has a lisp," Kay said, trying to ignore the others and focus on Alma, who never laughed much. Or even smiled much, for that matter.

"I guess I just don't see why it matters. Would it be better to have John Wayne as our priest? They're supposed to be married to the church anyway. Either way you go, they're supposed to keep their guns holstered."

Kay knew Alma had a point. And the thing was she wasn't even sure why she *did* care. She had no real problem with gays. Or sandals. Or toes. "I'm just being stupid. And old. Ignore me."

"I think you just miss Father M."

There was a wink in the way Alma said this, like she was saying something more than what she actually was. "Father M was a drunk."

"Maybe," Alma said. "But he was a good priest."

"A priest's priest."

Whatever Father M's faults or virtues were, the man had certainly liked his whiskey. And although Kay wasn't one to frequent Ruggers, she knew from both Norm and Douglas that their old priest had been there most nights they'd gone. *Father M was in fine form tonight, arguing pound for pound with Tate Barnes about the existence of God. Tate kept saying Father M's God was an insecure God, that he needed everybody to worship him and believe, that an all-knowing, omnipotent God wouldn't be insecure like that. He just wouldn't care is what Tate was saying. So Father M asks Tate if he cares about his children. And if he considers himself stronger and smarter than his children. And if he liked to hear his children tell him they loved him. You should have seen the red come over Tate's face.* It was one of the few times she'd ever heard Norm say something even remotely positive about the church.

Kay knew, without having to turn around, that the new priest had entered the room because the blue hairs had all quieted down and begun to sit up straight like good little girls when father came home. She found herself wondering lately if it mattered at all to this particular breed of follower what kind of man was behind the collar. Or was it simply the power of the collar that put them under such a spell? In a similar way as, say, people tend to become nervous and polite when speaking to police officers. Or doctors.

"Please help yourselves to more cookies, ladies. Don't be shy. If you don't eat them, the good Lord knows I'll polish them off myself later and we wouldn't want that."

A few of the ladies got up dutifully to get more cookies, and Kay rolled her eyes at Alma. "Be good," Alma said, nodding in the priest's direction. "Here comes Father Birkenstocks."

But the new priest wasn't wearing sandals that day. He had just given a sermon, on Daniel and the Lion's Den no less, and was stopping by after seeing his flock off. In other words, he was in his work duds.

"How did we do today, Alma? Enough for me to buy a Hummer?"

Alma gave Kay one of her deadpan looks that was clearly meant to shut down any plans Kay may have had to laugh outright at the comment. Which, of course, only made Kay want to laugh all the more.

"Oh, I'm sure you wouldn't really be interested in one those, Father."

"Wouldn't I?" he said, beaming at Kay now. "Might be fun."

"Well, I hate to disappoint you then, but it looks like we're more in the Honda Civic range today."

"Ah, well. Probably for the best."

With that, the priest strolled off to tend to the other hens. As the blue hairs spoke with him, Kay could almost taste the sugar that had come into their voices. Any diabetic within range would be in serious danger.

"I'm impressed you managed to hold your tongue, Catherine."

"I don't know what you're talking about."

"You looked like the whale with Jonah in its mouth."

"Nonsense. I don't even know what a hummer is."

"It's a car."

"Well, there you go."

They were nearly done. Kay reached into her coat pocket where she kept her digital watch but found the silver key instead. She didn't remember putting it there, but, then, that wasn't all that unusual these days. She thought of showing Alma the key, telling her how she had found it, but decided against it. She just wanted to go home now. Everything seemed so plastic there: the table, the laughter, the priest. She thought of Seven and imagined him snorting away there in the basement of the church, how magnificent and out of place he would be among all the fake. Just thinking about it gave her a little thrill.

Suddenly Kay changed her mind and set the key on the table. "I found this among Norm's things. But it doesn't fit anything in the house."

Alma merely raised her eyebrows at Kay, as if to say, "*So?*"

"It's a strange key, don't you think? Small, I mean."

"Looks like a P.O. box key to me. There a number on it?"

"No number."

"Maybe a safe deposit box?"

"I don't think Norm would even know how to go about getting one of those. Or have anything valuable enough to put inside."

"Value is usually defined by the valuer."

"Secrets are valuable."

Alma sat back in her chair, a rare smile on her face. "Catherine, what is going on with you?"

Kay told her about the book of matches she'd found from *Les Deux Magots*, that she knew it was silly to even give it another thought but that something didn't feel right.

"I don't know. You ask me, some things are best left unopened."

"You're probably right." Kay put the key back in her pocket. "I can't open what I don't have anyway, right?"

KAY HADN'T BEEN back to the repair shop since Norm died. She put all of that right on to Douglas. Which wasn't fair, but there was just no way she could have handled it. The shop was like a giant closet filled with Norm's clothes. Or like stepping into an urn. Even driving by it, something she had to do at least two or three times a week, was still difficult. She'd gotten good at not looking at the shop, pretending it wasn't there, but that was no good either.

As she entered, the radio Norm would play his "oldies" music on was now blaring something that, honestly, didn't sound much like music at all to Kay. But, then, she'd never understood what all the fuss had been about Elvis either. He'd never done a thing for her. Not even when he went religious. Maybe *especially* when he went religious.

She rang the buzzer by the entrance just like a customer would, and soon Marty appeared from around the corner of the office. She'd apparently caught him during a bathroom break.

"Mrs. O!" he said once he saw who it was. "I didn't know you were coming."

The way he was nervously wiping his hands on the rag hanging from his belt made Kay feel like a nun. A feeling she didn't like one bit. "It's just me, Marty. At ease."

"I know," he said, taking it down a few notches. "It's just, well, I haven't seen you around here since..."

"Since Norm passed. I know. I'm sorry about that."

She used the word "passed" for Marty's sake. He'd been close to Norm and the word, while annoying and inaccurate at best, was softer than "croaked." Which is what she'd nearly said.

"Douglas went out for a bit. I can get lost, too, if you want to be alone or something."

"That's nice of you, Marty, but I'm okay. Do you know where Douglas went by any chance?"

"He didn't say." Marty paused, like he was debating whether or not to say something. Then, "I'm pretty sure it has something to do with a girl. He tends to get secretive when he's seeing someone. Don't ask me why. It's not like anybody cares."

"Any guesses as to who?"

Marty shrugged. "Couldn't really say. I haven't been getting out all that much lately."

Kay knew that Marty's own father had abandoned him at a fairly young age. She'd heard about it from Douglas mostly, although she still didn't know all that much about it. And she knew that his father's absence was in no small way responsible for the bond he'd developed with her husband. Norm had given him the job, mentored him, so to speak. And she knew Marty had never forgotten that. She looked at Marty now, at his torn flannel, the smudges of grease along his cheek, and she saw pain. Kindness and pain and loss. She recognized this so clearly because it was how she felt, too. "You're a good kid, Marty. You know that, right? Norm thought the world of you."

Marty nodded, looked away the way men will do when they're trying not to get emotional. "I miss him," he said, staring at some tools hanging from a pegboard over the workbench. There were mason jars filled with nuts and bolts and washers, their lids bolted to the underside of the shelf because that was Norm. "I like being here, though. At the shop, I mean. It's almost like he's still here."

Kay was going to tell him that she understood. She was going to tell him about how she talked to Norm sometimes at home, that she was glad the shop was that kind of place for him, but the phone in the office started ringing and Marty left to answer it. Which, for a few moments anyway, left Kay alone in the shop to stare blankly at the wall of tools. It reminded her of an article she'd read once where Julia Child was explaining the best way to organize a kitchen. This, in a way, had been Norm's kitchen. There was even a soup-ladle-looking thing. And beside that some whisk-like something or other. She squinted her eyes so the tools blurred and blended together, the workbench transforming into the dirty Parisian kitchen of an absent chef. Even the deep smell of gasoline and WD40 now seemed like the workings of some mysterious broth brewing just out of sight. Kay stopped squinting, though, when she noticed something square and shiny on the top shelf.

"Sorry about that," Marty said from behind her, startling her. "Mrs. Cummings can't get her car started again. Doesn't want to pay for another tow either."

"Can't really blame her. You going to go get it?"

"Yeah, but not until later. She can wait."

Kay looked up at the hanging utensils again. "Do you know what that silver box is?"

"That? Not sure. It's just sort of always been there." Marty, without Kay having to ask, placed a stool in front of the workbench and climbed up. After wrestling the box out from under some old withered boxes and wiping some dust off, he handed it to Kay. "I bet it's sandpaper. He was always complaining about the sandpaper getting oily. He kept things like that in weird places, so Douglas and I couldn't get at them."

There was no handle to the box, no markings at all. Even the hinges seemed to blend in so as to be barely noticeable.

"Are we not opening it for some reason?"

Kay turned the box around so the tiny keyhole was facing Marty. "Not unless you have a key."

Marty looked at the box, then at the keys he kept on an old carabiner clipped to his jeans. "Hmm, I don't have anything that small. Douglas has Norm's old set of keys on him, I think. You could try those once he gets back."

"We'll see. It's probably just sandpaper like you said. I'll take it with me, though, just in case."

"If it's filled with gold you'll let me know, right? I could use a new sled."

"You'll be the first I call if I find any lightweight gold. I promise, Marty."

Back home, Kay set the silver box on the kitchen table and took the key from her coat pocket. It fit perfectly and when she turned it, the box made a little clicking sound before the top popped open. There was a messy stack of papers inside with an old photo sitting on top. The photo was the kind from her childhood with the white border along the outside, square, the size of the sticky notes she used for grocery lists. And there was Norm, standing outside the Louvre in his uniform, his hand wrapped around the waist of a woman. For a second, because of the black hair the woman had, Kay thought maybe it was her, that she had forgotten what she once looked like as a young woman. But it wasn't her. And even though the woman wasn't smiling, she seemed immeasurably happy. It was almost as if she were staring right at Kay, knowing someday she'd find her there, waiting, inside this stupid box.

Kay's hand was trembling. She went to the sink and rinsed out a glass. When she went to twist the cubes from the ice tray, the plastic cracked in a sharp, jagged line. That had never happened before, not once in thousands of ice cubes over the years. She dumped the cubes into the glass, pouring the whiskey in first, measuring it out like she used to do Norm's. Then the sweet vermouth. She was all out of bitters. She didn't care about bitters, though. She had enough bitters. Kay fished out a maraschino cherry from the jar and dropped it in the glass, using her finger to stir. Norm used to give Douglas a cherry now and then after he'd finished his drink. It used to bother her, but she'd never said anything. A lot used to bother Kay that she never said anything about.

She sat back down at the table and stared at the box and drank. She could lock it back up and swallow the key. One big gulp of her drink and it would be down the gullet. But then there'd be the bathroom to worry about later. It was a small key but not *that* small. She remembered the time Douglas swallowed a penny as a boy. He had been tilting his head back, balancing it on his nose when it slid down into his open mouth, and he accidentally gulped it down. At the time Kay hadn't known how serious a swallowed penny was and when Douglas had seen the look of horror on her face he immediately started screaming. She drove

Douglas to the hospital where they took some x-rays. The relief she'd felt when she saw that white circle resting in his stomach and not somewhere up near his sternum was enough to bring tears of relief. Which, of course, made poor Douglas think something was terribly wrong and so he'd started crying again. It was almost as if there were a direct conduit running between the two of them. Her happiness was his happiness, her pain, his pain, and so on. But things weren't like that anymore. Christ, she didn't even know where he was at the moment. Kay twisted the key in the lock absently. What if they were love letters to this woman in the photo? What if he'd had some secret life all this time she didn't know about? The lake. She could toss the key in the lake. She could toss the entire box in the lake and keep the key. She took another drink and felt the box softening at the edges, fading a little like the image in the old photo. That's when she got the nerve up to pull out the stack of papers and read the first poem.

My Heart Is Not a Flame
And you are not water
Or gasoline
My heart is the branch
Of a dark tree
A child's legs cycling
In the air like a sheet billowing
From an old clothesline
The Mercer sun fading the two of us
Second by wonderful

Second

SOMEWHERE HALFWAY INTO her fourteenth poem and her third Manhattan it started to rain. Kay wanted to go for a walk. How the idea got into her head, she wasn't exactly sure. But, once it had, it had taken root. She put on her Sorrels and her jacket, then remembered the raincoat Norm had gotten her that she'd never worn. It was one of those you could fold up to the size of a napkin and pack in a survival kit. Norm was always buying ridiculous things like that for her. She was certain there was a bunch of rich, old men living in mansions behind security gates somewhere who had made a fortune off selling these things to people like her husband. But, seeing as she couldn't find her real raincoat, Kay opted to drape the thin silver sheet around herself which, with the hood up, made her look like a walking bowl of *Jiffy Pop*.

Before heading outside, Kay made sure to pour the remainder of her Manhattan into the flask Norm thought he'd been hiding behind the cushion of the couch. There was still some whiskey left in it which tasted like fire. And fire was how she felt. Her head was one giant flame. *And my brain is the popcorn*, she muttered to herself and laughed as she went out the back door and into the rain. All those little and not-so-little aches and pains that followed her around during the day like needy children were gone now. She was free, if only temporarily. She patted the flask in her pocket as she walked. It was like a little portable gas tank.

Maybe she'd walk down to the flowage area. It was one of the places she and Douglas used to go together, back when he'd go on walks with her and they'd talk. She'd have to ask him to go on another with her. He was getting farther and farther away from her. Which was as it should be, but that didn't mean she had to like it much. She hoped he had a girlfriend, someone to talk to about his father. What was that old saying about two divorced people trying to date? Like two burn victims trying to hug. That's what she and Douglas were now. Two burn victims.

As she passed by Shawna's place, Kay saw Seven out in his pen, his great head lifting and snorting as she came into view. Kay walked right up to him so her face was even with his. She wasn't afraid now. Which was either due to her getting used to the horse or the whiskey burning in her belly. Either way, she reached out now and placed her hand on his nose the way she'd seen Shawna do. When the horse didn't startle, Kay eyed the house, noting that there were no cars in the driveway, no lights on. She lifted the latch on the gate and entered the pen, Seven side-stepping a little as she did. *Want to go for a walk? Want an old lady on your back?* Seven snorted and pawed at the ground a little. *I'll take that as a yes. Okay, okay, hold your horses. Let me see if I can manage this somehow.* Kay grabbed the plastic chair from outside the pen and set it as close to the horse as she could. *That's it. C'mon now. You just stand put, and I'll climb up here and...* Seven seemed both to understand what Kay was going to attempt and that it was a horrible idea, but he remained in place as she climbed up onto the chair and placed a hand on his mane and the other on his bare back. *Do you believe in God, Seven? Do animals believe in God? Is there some kind of horse God? Or is that a stupid idea?* Kay noted the flare of Seven's nostrils, the slight bulge in his eyes. She gave a pat to the flask in her jacket and then, as delicately as she could, laid herself across Seven's back while sliding her leg over. As she did this, the chair gave way, toppling into the mud below, which caused Seven to whinny and sidestep. *Am I too heavy for you?* Seven, as if to answer her question, took a few graceful steps around the pen once she righted herself. *Good. Good boy. Now that we've got that settled, have you even been to church? No? Well, you're aren't missing out on much. Maybe some toes. Do you like toes? Me neither. Not God's best design if you ask me. But then you know all about that.* Kay gripped Seven's mane and gave a kick to his side like she'd seen Shawna do. The horse snorted and made his way through the gate and a few seconds later, Kay found herself heading down her street in the rain, drunk, on the back of a horse.

CHAPTER NINE
Paris

DOUGLAS HAD BEEN working on a new sketch to show Jenna when Marty called. "What, the liquor store closed?"

"You need to meet me at the church as soon as you can. I need some help getting your mom and this horse back home."

"Horse? You sure you aren't drunk?"

"Sober as a church mouse. Just get here."

When Douglas got to the church, Kay was still sitting on top of Seven, though it looked like at any moment she was going to topple off.

"Mom? You okay?"

"Dougie? Oh, thank God. Will you please tell this young man that I'm perfectly capable of finding my way around Paris on my own and that I don't need a chaperone."

Douglas had seen his mom drunk before, but this wasn't that. She sounded like a different person. Deciding to ignore the Paris comment for the time being, Douglas slowly approached the horse and rider like one might a potential bridge-jumper.

"Marty's just trying to help. You know Marty. Do you think you might want to come down off the horse so we can get you home?"

He'd hoped mentioning Marty by name might help bring her around a bit, but no such luck. "I have to get to the Louvre. I'm meeting my Norman there."

Douglas and Marty exchanged glances. There was no amount of liquor in the world that could turn Mercer into Paris. "I'm afraid the Louvre is closed for the day. You could always go in the morning. I'm sure Norman will understand."

Seven seemed to be getting tired of the situation, too, moving sideways as he was now.

"It can't be closed. I'm sorry, but I don't believe you. I have to go now. Thank you for the concern, both of you, but true love waits for no woman."

With that, Kay gave a stern kick to Seven's side, but the horse, again seeming to sense that something wasn't right, refused to do anything more than turn around in a circle. Kay tried once more, using both feet this time, and Seven promptly spun back around in the other direction. "The museum isn't far from here. If this horse won't cooperate, I suppose I'll just have to walk."

Douglas felt his stomach drop as he watched his mom lean back and swing her leg over. Predictably, she over-swung and her butt came sliding off, slamming her down right into Marty's arms, toppling them both onto the pavement.

"Whoa there, big guy," Douglas said to Seven, trying to keep him from bolting. "We just want to get you back home." But Seven wasn't paying much attention to Douglas. He had started to back away from their sorry group, toward the steps of the church.

Once Kay got to her feet, she and Marty both seeming to have escaped the fall without major injuries, she approached the horse as matter-of-factly as one might a small dog. "What's the matter, sweetie? You hungry? Want another croissant?"

Douglas and Marty again exchanged glances. The closest croissants Douglas knew of were at the Burger King about forty miles from town. "Shouldn't we put a rope around him or something?"

"He wouldn't like a rope," Kay said. "Would you like a rope around your neck?"

Right about now? Yeah, that actually doesn't sound too bad.

"You have anything in your truck, Marty?"

"I might. Let me see."

While they waited, Kay cooed to the horse in something that sounded like made-up French. Douglas didn't know a whole lot of French, so he couldn't be sure.

"Zere, zere, mon ami. Pelu pelu a fromage. Oui? Oui. Come tale zoo? Merde, merde, merde. Zha ten. Oooo la la."

Marty returned holding a yellow tie-down that he'd

made a sort of noose with by cinching it at the ratchet. "What do you think?"

Douglas was surprised he didn't suggest using the winch on the back of his truck. "I think that'll strangle him."

Marty pulled it taut, the noose closing in on itself. "We could use the other end."

The other end wasn't much better, with its rubber-coated grapple hook, but there weren't any other options.

"Go ahead then," Marty said, handing it to Douglas.

"Me? I don't know anything about horses."

"And I do?"

Douglas let the tie-down hang by his side as he approached Seven. His mom was still mumbling French gibberish as she stroked the horse's neck.

"Par lay do zhan-may a vec mwha."

All Douglas could think about was how he was going to explain this to Shawna. Would she even believe him? Maybe best just to leave the French stuff out. "Mom, do you think you might be able to put this around his neck? So I can walk him home?"

Douglas held the tie-down out to her, but his mom just stared at it with this lost look on her face. "I'm sorry, but I have a date." She then started to walk off like she'd forgotten about the horse altogether, which seemed to be enough to break whatever invisible thing was holding them all there together. Seven shook his head from side to side, then, without much hurry, trotted off toward the church and down a path before disappearing into the woods.

"Welp," Kay said, stopping and digging a flask out from her jacket pocket. "I guess that's that."

"Whoa there." Marty eased the flask from her hand before she could manage a drink. "That's not going to help anything. Trust me, I know."

Kay looked Marty up and down and, somewhat haughtily, said, "I don't doubt that you do." Which Douglas somewhat loved. "I don't suppose you'd mind dropping me off at the Louvre since my friend has apparently abandoned me on the church steps."

Not one part of Douglas liked playing along with whatever this was, but if he wanted to get his mom safely back home, he didn't have much choice. "I can take you there. Ready to go then?"

"I just don't know what would happen if I didn't make it. I'd probably break the poor man's heart. He was a soldier in the war, you know, and has a very fragile heart because of it. That's what makes him such a wonderful poet. We're planning on settling down in Paris one day."

"He's a lucky man," Marty said and opened the door as Kay lifted up her silver raincoat like the hem of a dress and climbed in. Marty followed after, sitting as close to the passenger-side door as possible. Douglas had planned on keeping quiet until they got her safely back home, but then, just as they made it out onto the main road, he heard a long, somewhat tortured, *"Ohhhhh..."* It reminded him of how sometimes people in movies will wake up and groan after they've been knocked out with the butt of a pistol.

"Mom? You okay?"

"Douglas? What's happening here?"

He reached over and took her hand in his. "You're okay. We're just taking you back home."

"Back home? Where was I?"

"You don't remember being at the church?"

"Was there a wedding?"

Douglas could feel Marty looking over at him. "No, nothing like that. You sort of took Shawna's horse out for a ride."

"Sort of?"

"You totally took Shawna's horse out for a ride."

Kay swiveled in her seat, looked out the rear window. "Then where is he?"

"He sort of... He ran off."

"Oh, that's not good. I feel horrible."

"Seven will be okay. My guess is Shawna will be able to find him easily enough."

"She's going to hate me." Kay then turned and looked at Marty like she'd only just noticed him. "Hi, Marty."

"Hi, Mrs. O."

Kay cupped her hand so that it covered her nose and mouth and breathed into it. "Oh, well, that explains it."

"That reminds me," Marty said, reaching into his coat. "I think this belongs to you."

Kay sheepishly took the flask from him. "I suppose a little more couldn't hurt at this point." Kay tipped the flask back, coughed, then offered it to Marty.

"Sure, why not?" When he'd had a pull, Marty tucked the flask back into his pocket.

Soon the familiar wooden white signs nailed to the oak trees came into view. All of them were shaped like arrows and bore the residents' last names. Their house was the last one before the road dead-ended into a wall of black spruce.

"Isn't that Shawna there?"

Sure enough, Shawna was standing out in the middle of the road like she'd been waiting for them.

"I guess I'm in trouble now."

To Douglas, his mom sounded like a little girl. Which wasn't at all like the woman he knew. "No one's getting in trouble. I'll help explain what happened."

"How are you going to do that? I stole her horse and lost him."

"It'll be fine." Douglas got out of the truck first. Shawna looked completely stricken, like she'd been holding her breath and wouldn't let it out again until she knew Seven was okay. "He's somewhere near the church. My mom--"

"He's okay then? You saw him?"

"We did. He's fine."

Kay climbed out and looped her arm through Douglas's, leaning against him. She looked exhausted to Douglas.

"Well, I'm afraid this old woman went and did something really stupid."

Marty, never a big fan of the truth to begin with, grabbed the flask and handed it to Douglas. "What's stupid is not locking the gate on that pen. All Mrs. O did was have a few too many and try to find a runaway horse."

Shawna looked over at the pen, then at Kay. "That doesn't explain the chair in the pen."

"Marty, you're sweet, but that's not true. For some reason, I thought it would be a good idea to climb up on him and go for a walk through town. Shawna, I can't tell you how--"

"Where did you last see him?"

"By the church," Douglas said before his mom could answer. "But we lost him in the woods behind." Douglas hung his head a little. "We're really sorry. This isn't like my--"

"Isn't like what? It's like all white people. You think everything belongs to you. Well, my horse fucking doesn't. You understand that, old lady?"

Before Douglas or his mom could say anything, Shawna stormed off back to her house.

"It's okay," Kay said quietly. "She's right. It's okay."

"C'mon," Douglas said, wrapping his arm around her. "Let's get you inside before you catch pneumonia."

When the door shut behind them, Kay turned to him and, with her voice lowered, said, "I know this is the wrong thing to say right now, but, Douglas, I had so much fun. I'm sorry, but I did. That animal may be God himself."

"I don't think that's okay to say, Catholic-wise and all, but okay." Douglas led her into the kitchen and sat her down at the table. "I'm going to make you a BLT and you're going to sit there and eat it. Deal?"

"Deal."

After he got the bacon going, he noticed her digging through something on the table. "What's with the box?"

"I found it in the shop."

"I thought it looked familiar. What's in it?"

"Bits and pieces of your father."

Douglas just gave her a look as the bacon started to sizzle.

"Sorry. They're mostly poems. Or fragments of poems and things, I guess. You never saw your dad putting anything in it?"

"No. Poems? Seriously?"

"Seriously."

"Well, that explains why you were talking about poetry earlier."

"I was?"

Douglas walked over, peered down at the stack of loose papers and picked one up. On the back of an old shop receipt, it read:

The moon is none of your business

And everybody knows it

Douglas placed it back in the pile before picking up another, longer one.

After the war it was never anything

But theatre, a big noise

From the people

But I tried to pay attention

To the three dark men in my head

When I can't find good milk

I give them ice cream

Or big buttons of berries

And we don't mind the vultures
Just out of sight
Carving deer for brunch
Or the black bears keeping quiet
In the shade trees
These days I'm on the list
So I don't cry when they unlace
The half-cadavers bricking in
The winter rain
I plan on being a complete wreck
By departure

He handed the poem to his mother, shaking his head. "My God, who are you people?"

CHAPTER TEN
Shawna

SHAWNA TURNED THE radio up as she drove around town. All night there'd been the incessant knocking of her mother's voice telling her Seven was in trouble. Shawna tried to dismiss it as just her mother's paranoia, but it still worried her. Which is why she turned the music up. It was a pointless thing to do, like trying to drown out the sound of a jet plane, but she did it anyway, and by the time she finally gave up for the night and parked in the church lot, her mother's voice had gone quiet.

As Shawna sat in the dark staring out at the big wooden doors of the old church, she thought about Elmer and how she'd told him earlier that day about burning down the loon. He'd taken it better than she'd expected he would. There were no pouty comments about the "grease monkey" which is what he called Douglas when he was jealous. She figured things went well because just before she'd told him, they had been looking at a brochure she'd gotten for the school in Madison. She thought he'd make fun of it, how idyllic and fancy it all seemed, but he hadn't. She could tell he liked it. And she understood why. Each photo was like a beckoning finger, asking them to step right into a movie. This is what their lives could be like. Shawna knew the reality of it all would probably be much different, but it was still fun to dream. Especially with Elmer.

Shawna placed a handful of Lucky Charms on the hood of her car, Seven's favorite, just in case he came through there again. As she tried to get some sleep, she imagined Seven safely back home, happily munching away on his hay. "When I find you," she whispered to the dark, "I'm going to take you out on a run until you're sweating and your heart is about to burst from happiness."

CHAPTER ELEVEN
Kay

"How you feeling this morning, killer?" Douglas said as he sat down to breakfast, his plate heaping with eggs and bacon and sausage and hash browns.

"My head hurts. And my butt."

"And your pride maybe?"

"Pride? What's that?" Kay snagged a piece of his bacon. "Jesus, when's the last time you ate?"

Douglas shoveled a forkful of eggs into his mouth and, with his mouth purposefully full, said, "I'm not the one eating Manhattans for dinner."

Kay nodded and stared at the silver box still there on the table. She wondered if Douglas had looked through it any more last night after she'd gone to bed. She herself had only managed to get about halfway through them.

"Have you spoken with Shawna yet?"

"I just got up, Mom. When would I have spoken to her?"

"I don't know. I just thought maybe..."

"I'll call her in a few minutes, okay?"

Kay got up and peered out the front window. The pen was still empty. "You mean once you've finished eating that entire pig?"

She was about to ask him if they should try looking for Seven before he headed to the shop when Shawna pulled into their driveway.

"Did you find Seven yet?" Kay asked when she came into the house without knocking.

"Do you see him anywhere?" Shawna said irritably, looking about as tired as Kay felt.

"No," Kay said quietly.

Douglas grabbed his bag from the kitchen table, the one he kept his sketchbook in. "I can help you look after work if you want, but I have to get Marty and open up the shop right now."

"Look, somebody called and said they saw Seven tied to a tree outside a house. I'm pretty sure I know who it is, but I need somebody to come with me. And, well, seeing as this is all your fault, I nominate you."

Douglas looked like he was about to object, so Kay gave his arm a squeeze before he could. "She's right. It is the least I could do. And it's not like I have any big plans today, do I?"

"Just take it easy, okay? Promise me."

"I promise." She then turned to Shawna. "Just give me a few minutes to get myself together."

Kay, as she sat on the end of her bed putting her boots on, suddenly felt nauseous. She told herself it was from the hangover, but she knew that wasn't true. It felt like her brain had been raised a few inches on one side, the world tilted just slightly. When she sat up from tying her boots, she thought she might throw up. And why had she been putting her boots on? She stared out at the lake. The Scamp was there. The boat was there. So Norm wasn't fishing. Maybe Kay was going fishing? She heard a noise in the kitchen, the refrigerator door opening. Norm was rooting around in the fridge for something to eat, which meant she'd probably end up making him a sandwich. She sighed and stood up, the room still not quite right.

"You want a tuna sandwich? I think there's still some leftover in there," she said, knowing full-well she sounded irritated, but when she stepped out into the kitchen, Kay saw the girl standing there.

"I just wanted a soda. That okay?"

"Of course," Kay said, grabbing a chair to steady herself. "I'm sorry. I seem to be a little confused at the moment."

Shawna put the orange soda back in the fridge. "I'm sorry. I didn't mean to startle you."

Kay realized the girl was talking to her like she used to talk to her own mother. Like Kay was a child. And a very stupid one at that.

"You didn't startle me. I'm fine."

"Are you feeling okay now then?"

"I'm fine," Kay said again, going to the fridge and grabbing the soda for the girl. "Just the drinking catching up with me. Nothing to worry about. Shall we go?"

Kay was relieved the girl was there, relieved they were leaving the house. She felt things un-tilting a little. Even the fact that there was no need to make a tuna sandwich was something of a small relief. Shawna drove in silence for some time, which let Kay take in the scenery. And it still *was* scenery to her even though Douglas had once described Mercer as "tree, tree, tree, deer, tree, tree, tree, drunk" which was mostly true but like just about everything else, you had to pay attention. That's all prayer was really. Paying attention. So Kay had always tried to find one thing to treasure and hold onto during her day. Sometimes it was hard to find that one thing, but today that thing was Shawna. Kay would do whatever it took to make things right with the girl. If she'd let her.

At some point, Shawna pulled a piece of paper out of her pocket and handed it to Kay. "This is where Seven's at. Do you recognize the address?"

"No, should I?"

Shawna slowed the car and pulled off onto the side of the road. She left the engine running but didn't say anything more, just laid her head against the steering wheel and squeezed the rubber padding of the wheel. It was something Kay herself had done before. The squeezing was supposed to keep the tears back, but it never did.

"Whatever it is, you can handle it. I know that much about you."

The tears found their way out now, spilling down the

side of the girl's face. "I'm sorry. I'm a garbage can of a person. I just want my Seven back."

The words *garbage can* made Kay's heart flinch. And the way the girl said them, it was obvious she believed it though Kay couldn't understand why.

"I've been diagnosed with Alzheimer's," Kay blurted out. She hadn't meant to say it. She hadn't, in fact, told a single soul until now. Not Alma. Not even Douglas. And even though it might not have been the best thing to tell the girl right then, she hoped that sharing her dirty secret might somehow erase the idea of any garbage cans.

"Shit."

Kay laughed. "Yes. Shit."

The girl leaned back in her seat and wiped at her face. "I'm sorry for you and everything, don't get me wrong, but poor Douglas, too."

Kay dug in her coat pocket, handed the girl a small packet of tissues. "I know what you mean. But I don't worry so much because I can picture him later in life, with a family and his drawings and his quietness, and I just know he's going to be fine. I'm glad for that at least." Kay said nothing for a bit, just stared out at the road. There was a crushed Big Gulp container in the gravel, the plastic splayed out like a hideous fan.

"I wish my mom could have told me she was going to be murdered. I would have been able to tell her things, you know? It's good you and Douglas will have that."

"You're the only person I've told. I didn't really mean to. I'm honestly not sure why I did." Kay thought about Norm and whether knowing beforehand about his death would have changed anything. She knew instantly it wouldn't have. You say the things you need to say throughout a lifetime in the little things you do. Even so, she said, "I'll tell Douglas soon. I promise. I guess I'm still just getting used to the idea."

"How long do you have? I mean, before..."

"Before I lose my marbles?" Kay leaned over and patted the girl's knee when she didn't smile. "They say I'm getting toward the end of stage 3 if that means anything to you."

The girl nodded but said nothing. It was something Kay admired about the girl, her stoicism, but she also wished the girl could loosen up a little. What kind of pressure did a person have to be under to end up feeling like a waste can? Especially when the world was so full of other candidates better qualified for the label.

"So is there, like, anything they can do for it?"

"No, not unless somebody comes up with a cure. And I don't see that happening any time soon."

"So what are you going to do?"

"Die."

The girl, obviously not intending to, laughed at this and then quickly covered her mouth. "See... garbage can."

"Stop it. If you can't laugh at times like this then you're already dead. Am I right?" The girl nodded. "Okay, that's enough of that then. How about it's your turn now and you tell me what you were crying about?"

"The house we're going to is Peyton Crane's. He's the one that has my horse. Do you know who he is?"

"I do. He's just a big bully. I'm sure the two of us can handle him just fine, don't you think?"

Shawna smiled, wiped at her tears. "It's not him I'm worried about. He was friends with my step-dad. Good friends. So I sort of have an obsession with him. And not the good kind."

"And you're worried you might do something bad?"

The girl nodded. It was obvious she didn't want to say anything more, so, instead of pushing her, Kay said, "I'll keep a close eye on you, don't worry. And I know you want to get your horse, so let's say we do that, okay?"

"Okay," the girl said.

They drove on and after a few minutes, Shawna slowed the car and stopped in the middle of the road. There, at the end of the street, was a horse standing in the front yard of a small red house.

"Is there a problem?"

Shawna took her foot off the brake and started toward the house. "No."

Kay kept quiet, trusting that Shawna could handle herself no matter what situation they were walking into. As they parked and got out of the car, Seven began pawing at the ground and snorting. It reminded Kay of a dog wagging its tail.

"Aren't you going to knock on the door?"

Shawna took her time untying the rope that had been placed around Seven's neck. "That's probably not a good idea."

Kay looked at the house, tried to see if there was

anything menacing about it, but it looked like just about any other house around there. There was a pick-up in the driveway, a toy shotgun resting in a bed of foxgloves by the front door. She watched as Shawna stroked Seven's nose, calming him.

"Would you mind giving me a hand real quick, so I can mount him?" When Kay looked at her skeptically, Shawna interlaced her fingers and held them out. "Just keep your back straight, and you'll be fine. I'm not all that heavy."

Kay smiled at the girl. "My back hasn't been straight in years, but, okay, I'll try."

As Kay hunched over, Shawna carefully placed her foot in the web Kay was making with her hands, placing one hand on Seven's back and the other on Kay's shoulder. Then, in one fluid motion, she swung up onto Seven. Kay was about to ask if she should follow them back home when the front door of the house opened.

"Can I help you?"

There in the doorway stood a bearded man in overalls. A not-uncommon sight in Mercer, but there was something about the man that Kay immediately disliked. When Shawna just stared at him, Kay took it upon herself to answer for her.

"You seem to have found her horse. We're just taking him back home now. Thank you."

The man seemed about to say something when a little boy came running out of the house, pushing past him. "Hey, that's my horsey!"

Instead of correcting the boy's claim, Kay thought she could see a wry smile creep out from under the man's beard.

The boy, like the father, gave Kay the impression that he lived under the house rather than in it. His brown hair was unusually long for most boys in town and shot out in all directions. Which could have been endearing on most other children, Lord knew Douglas looked similar at that age, but Kay found herself feeling sorry for the boy instead. At the sight of him, Seven took a few quick steps back, seemingly just as repulsed by the little ball of dirt as Kay.

"I said that's my horsey!"

Shawna regarded the boy a moment then gave Seven a little kick and guided him toward the man in the doorway. As she did so, the boy called out, "Indian giver!"

Shawna simply turned and smiled at the boy like he'd just said something adorable. The boy, obviously confused by her reaction, said it again. "Indian giver!"

Kay found herself transfixed, not for the first time, by Shawna sitting there atop Seven. They were like one word, something fluid and written by a steady hand: *FuckOff*. The man in the doorway took a step forward as Shawna and the horse approached, almost as if he was determined to stop them from entering the house.

"You got papers for that animal? How we supposed to know he's yours?"

Shawna regarded the man not much differently than she had the boy. "Do you know who I am?"

The man turned his head and spit in the grass. Men. Always posturing. What a tiny specimen he seemed alongside Shawna and Seven.

"You're Ayasha's girl. So?"

Shawna turned her head and spit and it took everything Kay had not to clap. The smirk that came across the man's face was sickly. "That's right. Ayasha's girl. And I know exactly who you are."

The man turned his head like he was going to spit again but thought the better of it. "Fine, I'll bite. Who am I then?"

Shawna looked at the boy who was now pouting and close to tears, realizing, no doubt, that soon his *horsey* would be gone. "Peyton Crane. Owner and proprietor of Treaty Beer. And best friend to Stephen Bessmer."

The man smiled up at Shawna, and again Kay saw the rotten scrawled therein. "That's me. What of it?"

Shawna turned to the little boy. "You like Spider-Man?"

The boy looked up at his dad like maybe he needed permission to answer. When his father nodded, the boy said, "Yeah, I like him okay. Why?"

"No reason. I used to like him, too, is all."

"But you don't anymore?"

"Oh, I don't know. I guess I still like him."

"He can shoot webs from his hands to catch the bad guys."

"That's right. You just have to know who the bad guys are."

"That's easy."

"Yeah? How can you tell?"

"They always look dirty and wear black and sometimes bandanas."

Shawna nodded. "In comic books maybe, but in real life, it's not so easy to figure out sometimes."

"But I can tell."

"Am I a bad guy then?"

Kay watched as the boy looked back up at Shawna and, after a few seconds, begrudgingly shook his head from side to side.

"And you know this is my horse, don't you?"

"Yeah, I guess so."

"That's good," Shawna said, smiling down at him. "Keep doing that, thinking for yourself. That's what Spidey always did."

Without so much as giving the father another glance, Shawna turned Seven around and brought him over to where Kay was standing. "Don't ever get on my horse again. Understood?"

"Understood. I'm sorry about all this."

"I know you are. We're good."

Kay got back into her car and backed out of the driveway. She stopped and watched the man, a scowl still on his face, making sure he didn't try to follow them. The boy had his back to the man, busy as he was watching Shawna and Seven disappear down the road. Then the man said something to the boy that Kay couldn't hear, but the boy turned, the unmistakable look of fear spreading across his face as he hung his head and headed back inside the house.

CHAPTER TWELVE
Douglas

D OUGLAS SAT IN the Scamp trying to sketch Jenna's face, but his hands were trembling from working on the steps. It happened some days after working at the shop, too, all that clenching and squeezing of big dumb things made it nearly impossible for him to manage the thinness of a simple pencil. And so, after barely managing an eye, he gave up and laid down on the bunk. He could hear someone out on the lake fishing, an old boat groaning and creaking its way across the water like a rusty echo. Someone cracked open a can of something and Douglas found himself imagining the lake drained of water, how deep the center of it would be, then, over time, covering over with ryegrass, reincarnating itself as a field, the fish turning to wildflowers, the docks all lying down like so many bones littering a vibrant grave. Would it feel different being down there? Would you somehow still feel the water around you? Would you find yourself having trouble breathing? Douglas closed his eyes and listened to the lake, all that dark life going on just under the surface. It was like a neighbor you could hear but only ever saw passing glimpses of.

As he drifted off to sleep, Douglas could see Jenna's mouth, the way her lip sometimes curled when she smiled. His father's death was there the night he'd slept with her. It was there in the room, and then it was inside Douglas, and then it was inside Jenna. Douglas didn't quite know how to explain that, creepy as it sounded, but he knew it was true just the same.

Later, a knock at the door woke Douglas from a dream he was having where Seven had become human. Human Seven had become a big drinker and basically lived at the bar and never stopped talking about the Packers.

"Douglas, honey, you in there?"

His mom poked her head in, her eyes averted like maybe she expected him to be naked. Or worse. She did the same thing whenever she came into his bedroom though he'd never given her any reason to do so. "Can I talk to you in the house for a second? Whenever you're done out here, of course."

Douglas slid his notebook under the covers and hopped down from the bunk. "Is something wrong?"

"No, I just want to talk for a bit."

As they walked up to the house, Douglas found himself piecing his dream back together. Jenna had been at the bar talking to Human Seven and was laughing at all his stupid jokes. And Seven would laugh, too, his big horse-teeth angling out of his mouth as he did. Douglas had just sat there at the bar watching how she put her hand on

Human Seven's thigh and kept looked down there, like she was checking to see if that area was horse or human-like. Human Seven had been wearing this thick leather necklace which, once he'd had his fill of whiskey, Jenna had grabbed hold of like reins after hopping on his back, then the two of them trotting right out of the bar and laughing all the way while Douglas just sat there doing nothing. The dream had left a sick feeling in his stomach.

Once inside, Kay sat across from him at the kitchen table. Douglas swore he could hear ice cubes tinkling in the living room; it took him a few seconds to realize it was just something coming from the TV and not one of his dad's Manhattans.

"I miss Norm," Kay said, and Douglas wondered if she'd heard it too.

"I know you do."

It was the first time she'd said anything of the sort since his dad died. It felt strange just hearing his name spoken aloud.

"You know you don't have to stay in Mercer. Your old mother will be just fine if you leave."

Douglas wasn't sure where any of this was coming from. And he didn't think she was *just fine*. Neither of them were.

"What would we do about the shop?"

"Maybe it's time we put the shop to rest as well. We could sell, use the money so you can go to college. Maybe take some real drawing classes. I don't know."

"No." Douglas got up, poured himself a drink. He then poured another for her and jangled the cubes around.

The sound was comforting. "I'm not leaving Mercer. I like running the shop. I'm good at it."

"Just because you're good at something doesn't mean you have to keep doing it."

"I know."

"Fine," she said and took the drink from him. "Just promise me one thing."

"What's that?"

"Don't become the shop like your father did. Don't hide your dreams inside a silver box. Or a sketchbook. Oh, I don't know, just live your dreams before it's too late."

"Okay," he said, still not sure where all this was coming from. "But I'm still not going anywhere."

"You know I'd keep you here with me forever if I could."

"We'd become alcoholics."

Kay raised her glass. "Funny."

Outside the wind was acting up again, the trees all bending and bowing in the half-light.

"I'm almost finished with the steps," Douglas said, but his mother only nodded absently. She was looking out the window, at the fading outline of the lake.

"I swear the days are getting shorter and shorter."

"Mom?"

"Yes, dear?"

"Did you hear me?"

"I'm sorry. That's good, honey. Real good."

WHEN SHAWNA'S NAAN opened the door, Douglas immediately regretted bringing his drink with him. The old lady mumbled a glum hello and let him in before disappearing back inside the house, presumably to get Shawna though she made no mention of this. He'd only been in the house a handful of times and each time he was struck by how un-Indian it seemed. Which was probably racist on some level, and never something he would actually mention to Shawna (which probably meant it *was* racist), but her home wasn't all that much different from his own. There was even a TV on too loud and while he couldn't be sure, he thought it might be *Matlock*. When Shawna eventually came into the kitchen, she was wearing sweatpants and a tank-top, like maybe she'd been sleeping.

"You here to steal something of mine too?"

"Yeah. That okay?" She rolled her eyes at him and grabbed a hoodie off a hook by the door. This was their normal routine; they never stayed in her house for long. "Seven doing okay after his adventure?"

"No signs of having contracted bigotry yet." When Douglas just stared at her, she said, "Your mom didn't tell you?"

"No, but she's been acting strange lately. Have you--?"

"Peyton Crane had him."

"You're shitting me."

Shawna shook her head. "I hate that expression.

Anyway, yeah, she drove me. A friend had spotted him and gave me the address."

"That must have been hard."

Shawna gave him a quick look that said *You have no fucking idea how hard,* and they walked over to his house and down to the dock. Lights from the houses across the lake reflected gold off the water as Shawna kicked off her shoes and dangled her feet from the end of the dock. Douglas offered her some of his drink, but she refused.

"So do you want to talk about it or no? The Peyton Crane thing, I mean."

Shawna was quiet for a bit, then, "Not much to say. He's a pig. No, scratch that. I actually kind of like pigs. He's a human."

Douglas took a seat on the bench behind her, which was where he usually sat. His dad had built the bench, bolted it to the sinking dock. In another year or so, the entire thing would be submerged if he didn't take care of it soon. What the point was of salvaging it, though, he wasn't quite sure. He watched as Shawna dug out a stray bottle cap lodged between the planks and tried skipping it across the water, but it just arced and nosedived into the lake.

"Have you seen that woman from the coffee shop again?"

"Last night, actually. I think I might like her."

"You do like her, dummy." Somebody on the other side of the lake screamed, a happy scream, a child being chased by a silly grown-up monster, but the sound of it seemed to jolt Shawna out of something. "So I need to tell you something. And it's not going to be easy to hear."

Douglas, trying to find the source of the giggles splintering out across the water, almost hadn't heard Shawna. When it did finally register, he said, "Okay. Go ahead."

Shawna was looking at him strangely, almost like she was frightened of something, and then pivoted so that she was facing him straight on, hugging her knees to her chest. There was more squealing from across the lake, more tinned voices. "It's your mom. She told me something today that I don't think you know about."

"Just tell me."

"She has Alzheimer's. I'm sorry."

There was more laughter which now seemed to be racing across the water at him. It was a young girl's laughter. Maybe a sibling being chased. Douglas could feel the lake evaporating, could feel himself at the bottom of it, in that field he'd been imagining, fresh air all around him but not able to breathe an ounce of it.

HE WAS FAIRLY well lit by the time he knocked on Jenna's door.

"You're drunk."

"You're right."

"Okay. You'd better come in then, I guess."

The living room seemed smaller somehow than he remembered it. The dog, Shredder or Shedder, he couldn't remember which it was now, was sitting on the couch wagging his tail, too lazy, apparently, to get up. Douglas sat down next to the dog, letting him slobber on his hand before Jenna pulled him off. "Easy, Shredder. Save some for Mama."

The painting of the wheelchair was nowhere to be seen now. In its place on the easel was a large sketch pad, an unfinished pastel drawing of a white-tail deer blooming out of it. "You've been infected by Mercer, I see. Next, it'll be a pike or loon."

"Um, I've already tried a loon."

"Well, there you go. And?"

"And it needs work. Don't underestimate the loon, Douglas. There's a reason people are fascinated by them."

"Yeah? Why's that?" He was trying to sound cool and indifferent but was quickly realizing he sounded more like a dick than anything else.

"They're...well, they're magical."

"Yeah, you definitely aren't from here."

Douglas had brought his sketchbook with him this time but had chickened out at the last minute and left it in the car. He pulled out his father's flask, the one his mother had taken to using, and took a pull.

"You think that's a good idea?"

Jenna said this gently, her voice as soft and kind as any he'd ever heard. He could listen to her read the Bible or even one of Marty's fishing mags, and it would still sound like a song to him. He was hooked. Good and deep. "Better get the needle-nose," he mumbled to himself, "rip out my esophagus."

"Okay, definitely *not* a good idea. Why don't you give me that, and I'll put on some coffee."

Douglas took another quick hit off the flask but then handed it over. "I like you, you know. A lot."

"You're just drunk. *A lot.* But thank you. I like you back."

When Jenna disappeared into the kitchen, Douglas made up his mind to show her the drawings. If he didn't do it now, he knew he probably never would. He stumbled his way out to the car with an anger and sadness mixing themselves up inside him that made him feel cut wide open. When he got back inside, there was Jenna sitting on the couch with Shredder's head in her lap, a cup of coffee steaming away on the table. "It's nothing fancy. I hope that's okay."

"It's more than okay. Thank you," he said and sat down, handing her the sketchbook. "I'm going to drink this and pretend you aren't looking at those, okay?"

Jenna began to slowly turn through the pages, stopping over some longer than others. It took everything Douglas had not to peer over and see which ones had caught her interest.

"If you're hungry, I have leftovers in the fridge."

She said this nodding to the fingers he'd begun to chew on. He put his hands at his side, suddenly realizing just how ridiculous a thing it was to show her his drawings. He was about to ask for them back, apologize for coming there drunk, when she closed the book and gently set it on her lap. "Ready for your critique?"

"Yeah," he said, trying to sound sober. "No."

"Well, you're going to get laid tonight even though you smell like the wrong end of a plunger."

Douglas wondered if his mom was still snoring away on the couch. The image of her there with her mouth hanging open flashed through his mind. "Does that mean they're good, or do you have a thing for plungers?"

Jenna flipped through the book until she found the one she wanted and held it up for him to see. It was the one of the loon with the broken neck. "This doesn't look like anything I've seen before. It's different. It's not always about how well you can draw something, right?" She caught the look he was giving her. "I don't mean that in a bad way. You can definitely draw. Think of it like a song. You know how you can hear someone with a pitch-perfect voice, but their singing doesn't move you at all? Well, drawing is pretty much the same thing. Think Mick Jagger. Tom Waits. You think they'd get laid without having style?"

Douglas's mouth was dry. His tongue felt like a loaf of bread. One of those fat European kinds. He'd never been with a woman who talked like this. When she spoke, she twisted something over inside him, like she was looking under all the rocks of him. The *underside* of him. The phrase worked its way into his head all on its own and while he didn't exactly know what it meant, he knew it described the feeling perfectly.

"But you like Seven," he mumbled, thinking he was being funny.

"Um, what?"

He looked over at her, but she wasn't smiling even a

little. "Nothing," he said stupidly. "I had a dream about you, that's all."

"Okay, so now you have to tell me."

He remembered something somebody had told him once about people only wanting to hear your dreams if they were about them. Which was most likely true, though maybe not in this case. "Maybe later, okay? I think I need some more of this coffee first."

Jenna got up and put some music on, a band Douglas wasn't familiar with, but that wasn't all that unusual. The song was slow, atmospheric, like the guitar had been dipped in hangover. Douglas watched her sway to the music with her back to him.

"You want to see what I used to do, don't you? But you're too shy to ask."

When she turned to look at him, Douglas nodded, which was pretty much all he was capable of doing besides drooling right along with the dog.

"Okay, hold on. It's been a little while so I might be rusty." He watched as she dug through a closet by the front door and returned holding a long, black scarf. "I'm used to a pole, so we're going to have to improvise a little." There was a potted plant of some kind hanging from the ceiling which she took down before tying the scarf to the hook so that it dangled there like a long silk snake. "Ready?" She lit a candle on the coffee table, then dimmed the lights before skipping a few songs ahead. When she slid off the sweat pants she'd been wearing and was down to just a pair of black panties, she turned to Douglas and somewhat shyly said, "Not fair just me showing you everything, is it?"

She bent over, sliding the panties down to her ankles. "Please," she said in a pouty voice, and Douglas unbuckled his jeans and kicked off his shoes. When he stood and took them off, his junk bobbing there dumbly in front of him, she smiled that crooked smile of hers at him.

"Good boy." She sat down in a chair across from him with her legs closed. "Now sit down, okay?"

Douglas, of course, did as he was told.

"Do you want to see?" she purred, rocking her thighs from side to side with her hands resting on her knees.

Douglas nodded, the loaf of bread in his mouth expanding.

"If I do, will you touch yourself for me?"

Again, Douglas nodded. She could ask him to saw off his arm right now and he'd nod yes. Who was this woman? Did other men have girlfriends who did this sort of thing for them? Maybe, he figured, but definitely not someone with legs like Jenna's. Not in Mercer, anyway. When Douglas took hold of himself, she got up and made her way to the bathroom. When she came back, she carefully laid a towel on the floor in front of him. "Don't worry, it'll turn me on if you just let yourself go."

When Jenna sat back down and slowly opened her legs for him, Douglas no longer felt inside his body. Or maybe he felt *entirely* inside his body. He wasn't sure. Every single emotion and sensation was fused together now. He was both absent and extremely present, like he was floating somewhere up above, watching both himself and Jenna. He could feel himself tiptoeing to an edge, then stepping back, his whole body condensed and pulsing. But even as he watched Jenna slide her fingers between her legs, even as she moaned and whimpered for him, the shadow of why he had gotten drunk in the first place hovered there around him, too.

"What's wrong?"

"Nothing. Why?"

"Well..." she said, nodding toward his hand. "You seem a bit, um, distracted."

Douglas looked down, saw that he'd gone soft. "Shoot," he said. "It's just the whiskey. I'll be fine in a minute."

Jenna got up, walked over to him and knelt before him. "It's not just the whiskey," she said. "Something's obviously bothering you. We don't have to talk about it tonight if you don't want to, though."

"Will you do something for me?"

"It depends," she said playfully.

Douglas stood up. "It's nothing weird. Wait, yes, it's totally weird." Douglas kicked his jeans fully off then squatted down with his back to her. "Hop on. I want to give you a ride."

"You're kidding, right?"

"C'mon, it'll be fun. Trust me."

"Famous last words." Jenna placed her hands on his shoulders. "I've seen a lot of stuff before, but, yeah, this is a new one for me."

She hopped onto Douglas's back, her legs wrapped around his waist as he hoisted her up and started moving about the living room at something like a trot.

"Giddy up," Douglas called out and Jenna started to laugh.

"Wait, wouldn't you be the horse in this scenario?"

"Oh, right. Ha."

The novelty of the situation soon wore off, though. Mainly because drunk horses, it turned out, had weak thighs and couldn't carry riders for very long no matter how light and sexy they were. So Douglas carried them into the bedroom, collapsing them onto the bed.

"You're a strange one, Douglas. Lucky for you I'm a big fan of strange."

With her legs still around his waist, she kissed him. And the kiss, the way her lips lingered before slowly pulling away, was full of dirt, layers and layers of it and he couldn't get enough. He wanted to do everything all at once to her. That's what it felt like.

"You're a nice combination," she said when she pulled away from him.

"What does that mean?"

"I don't know. Both sweet and dirty, I guess."

"Then that's a good thing?"

"It's a very good thing."

CHAPTER THIRTEEN
Shawna

SHAWNA WAS ABOUT to head out to the back porch for her nightly stalking when she heard her naan snoring in her mother's old bedroom. They'd kept the house after the murder. Her step-dad's side of the family insisted on it, said it was the least they could do. Shawna hated living there, but they'd be leaving next year if everything went as planned. Shawna poked her head in the door, watched her naan's chest rising and falling. Her naan was magic. When they found out about it, she held Shawna in her arms for hours and sang all kinds of songs to her. And not just Ojibwa songs. She sang the Beatles and Neil Young and even some Neil Diamond. But they all sounded Indian the way her naan sang them in her low husky voice, the rhythm sort of jumping in slow motion. Her naan was medicine. Elmer was medicine. Seven was medicine. And all of that medicine still seemed like it was barely enough to keep her from getting sick. And there were so many ways for people to be sick. Shawna saw it everywhere. In town.

On the reservation. At the casino. So much of it that she'd come to think of the world as an open-aired hospital ward, everyone shuffling around in their hospital gowns, lugging around invisible IVs, carrying on as best they could. When her naan's time came, Shawna didn't know how she was going to handle it. Just the thought of it made her throat close up. But if she'd learned anything so far it was that we don't handle death: death handles us.

The first month after it happened Shawna didn't eat much. She felt like a rag doll. Like a rag doll without rags. And on those rare occasions when she was around other people, she found herself filled with the irrepressible urge to spit on them. She never did it, of course, though she remembered spitting on the ground once uncomfortably close to some people passing by. She still had the urge some days. And there had been the voice of her mom floating in and out of her head. Talking. Always talking.

"Shawna, eat for me please."

"Love yourself for me, baby."

"You're making me cry. Don't make your mother cry."

And her naan bringing her fry bread, potato chips, ice cream, grilled cheese with turkey, mac and cheese, hot dogs... anything to get Shawna to eat. And she did eat eventually. Just enough to put a few rags into the doll. Which were more like tissues than rags: flimsy things propping her up inside just enough to get through the day. Just enough to appease the incessant voice of her mother.

Shawna went out to the back porch and sat in the rocking chair her naan liked to nap in, putting her feet up on the railing. The lights were out across the lake.

Which meant he was either asleep already or still at the bar. Normally this was would have bothered Shawna, the not knowing, but tonight it didn't. She pulled the brochure out from her pocket and, under the starlight, tried to imagine herself studying at a coffee shop in Madison, Elmer sitting across from her smoking a cigarette, not a slot machine in sight.

CHAPTER FOURTEEN
Kay

WHILE IT WAS true Kay sometimes forgot what day it was, or why she had come into a certain room, it was also true that lately other memories were vividly flooding back. She was sitting on the couch reading one of Norm's poems about a fish when one such memory resurfaced. She hadn't thought about it in years but now she could see herself lingering outside a young Douglas's door, listening as Norm told him a bedtime story..

Once upon a time there was a little fart.

No...

Sorry. Once upon a time there was a little boy who went fishing.

That's me.

Maybe. And this little boy was minding his own business, just trying to catch a fish on the lake behind his house, when suddenly he felt something tug at his line. And it wasn't just any kind of normal tug. The boy's pole bent nearly in half from the weight of whatever was under the surface of the water.

Probably a whale. I bet it's a whale.

But just then a whale popped his head out of the water and said, "I'm not a whale!" and then disappeared back under the water.

Aww, but I wanted it to be...

Doug.

I'll be quiet.

So just as the boy was wondering if his pole was going to break, the line went completely slack. The boy, thinking he'd lost the fish, slowly began to reel his line back in. He reeled and reeled, but there seemed to be no end to the line. What had happened to his hook and worm? And where was all this extra line coming from? The boy, his arms now starting to hurt from all the reeling, eventually had to stop because his spool couldn't hold any more. Baffled, he set his pole down in the boat and stared out across the water. It was quiet out, not a ripple on the water, and the boy was thinking about cutting the line and going back home when he thought he heard something scratching along the bottom of the boat...

Don't make it too scary. Sometimes you make it too scary.

A little scary is okay, though, right?

Yeah. Just a little.

Okay. So the little boy...

And could you maybe stop calling him little? Maybe he's not as little as people think.

Fair enough. Okay, so the sound, the scraping sound on

the bottom of the boat kept getting louder and louder, like the boat was dragging against the bottom. But that couldn't be because the boy, a very mature boy for his age, knew he had dropped anchor right in the middle of the lake. Just then the boat started rising out of the water. Only a little bit at first, like there was a giant hand under the water carefully lifting the boat out of the water to inspect it. The big boy sat down and gripped the bench seat with both his hands. He was about to call out for help, maybe yell for his mother, when the boat slowly settled back into the water again. But the boy couldn't move now. He felt glued to his seat, frozen there so that even if he wanted to move, he couldn't.

I don't like this part. Does it get better soon?

It'll get better. Just wait.

Okay.

Then the line on the boy's pole started running out again, racing out over the side of the boat, threatening to carry the pole and spool and everything over the side. The boy lunged for the pole, grabbing it just as it was about to be dragged into the water. And suddenly the boy wasn't afraid anymore. He knew what he had to do: he had to catch whatever it was that was pulling on that line. He set the drag on the spool and then grabbed the reel tight in his hands so that the line stopped running. When he looked out over the water, there, not twenty feet from the boat, he saw the back of a monster-sized sunfish breach the surface. But it wasn't just any sunfish. This sunfish really did look like an actual sun. Its scales were a fierce yellow that seemed to burn there in the water, and little bubbles erupted all alongside the fish like maybe the water was boiling.

Cool.

The boy thought it was cool, too, although he had no idea how he could reel him in without burning a hole in his fishing line. Even so, he started reeling, and, much to his surprise, he found that the sunfish wasn't all that difficult to bring in. It seemed, in fact, to be swimming toward the boat rather than away. Faster and faster the boy reeled the line in and soon the giant fish was there beside his boat. As the boy stared in awe at the fish, wondering if it would burn a hole through his net, or worse, through the hull of the boat, the fish smacked the water with a fin, splashing water on the boy's face. "What's the matter with you?" the fish said to the boy. "Aren't you going to invite me in?" The boy was stunned. He'd never seen a talking fish before.

Only in cartoons.

Exactly. Only in cartoons. The boy kicked his tackle box across the floor of the boat with his foot to make room for the fish, already planning in his head how he'd bring the fish back home and introduce him to his mom.

I'd show him to you, too.

"Please," said the boy timidly, "come into my boat. I won't hurt you." The fish laughed at this. "You won't hurt me? Ha. How about I won't hurt you?" The boy didn't know what to say to this, but he could see that the fish was right: if he were to touch it, there was little doubt he'd get burned badly. So, with a quick twist and arch of his body, the fish jumped from the water and into the boat causing the boat to rock back and forth violently as if a giant wave had struck it.

"Well," the fish said, his scales shimmering with heat, "are you going to remove this thing from my mouth or what?"

The boy had been so awestruck by the fish that he hadn't

noticed the hook through its upper lip. "Oh," said the boy. "I'm so sorry. Hold on a second and let me see what I can do." Nervously, the boy rummaged through his tackle box and pulled out an old pair of needle-nose pliers.

The ones you gave me.

The fish scooted back a little in the boat. "Easy there, fella. You sure you know how to work those?" The boy lied and told the fish he was an expert hook remover. The truth, however, was that the boy had mangled a few mouths in his short career as a fisherman, not to mention the countless esophagi he'd accidentally ripped from the throats of innocent fish who had been unfortunate enough to swallow one of his hooks.

What kind of guy?

Esophagi. I'll explain later. So, not knowing any better, the massive talking sunfish scooted closer to the boy, offering up his lip to him. As the boy carefully set about removing the hook from the poor fish's lip, he noticed a hole in the side of the fish. When he looked closer, he saw that it went clear through the sunfish.

"Dibbn't any slubby eber smell you it boob poo slare?"

The boy, realizing the fish couldn't speak very well with the pliers in his mouth, removed them and the fish tried again.

"Didn't anybody ever tell you it's rude to stare?"

"I'm sorry," said the boy. "It just looks so painful. What happened to you?"

The fish then told the boy a strange story about a giant metal stick bursting through the water and nearly cutting him in two. "I was lucky. If I had been a few inches to one side or the other, I wouldn't be here right now talking to you."

"But what was it?" the boy asked.

"At the time I didn't know what it was. But later I found out it was called a spear. Some people were trying to kill a different kind of fish, what you call Walleye, but it accidentally hit me."

"Wow," the boy said, "you got really lucky."

The fish laughed, and rays of sunlight scattered out from his mouth. "You call a hole in my side and a hook in my mouth lucky?"

The boy wagged his head apologetically and returned to the work of removing the hook. After a few minutes of extremely careful tugging and twisting, the hook released itself from the fish's mouth, leaving only a small hole. "I'm sorry about that," said the boy. "Will you be okay?"

The fish gulped down some air, making big Os with his mouth, almost like he was imitating a normal fish. "What, this? Oh, I'll be fine. It kind of goes with the other one, don't you think?"

But the boy was too busy trying to figure out how to keep the fish to answer him. Maybe he could just row back with the fish there like he was. But just as the boy was starting to reach for the anchor line to pull it up, the fish gave a giant slap with his tail and launched himself into the air. Seeing that the fish was trying to escape, the boy lunged and tried to grab hold of it, but the fish was too smart for that and raised his dorsal fin just as the boy was reaching for him. "Ouch!" yelped the boy and pulled his hand back as the fish made a giant splash and disappeared under the water.

When the boy looked at his hand, however, he didn't see blood like he thought he would. Instead, there was a long black line across his palm, and suddenly the boy realized what had happened. He'd been burned by the fish, his hand scorched. The boy felt himself starting to cry, but, just as the first tear was about to fall, the big sunfish popped his head up out of the water.

"Sorry about that, kid. It was nothing personal. I had to stop you. You understand that, right?" The boy sniffled a little and nodded. "Look at this way," the fish went on. "Now you have something to remember me by. I don't know of any other human who's gotten close enough to touch me. You should think of that mark on your hand as a badge of honor, the scar of a true warrior. A true fisherman. Will you promise me you'll do that? That you'll be proud of it?"

The boy cradled his hand and smiled down at the fish. "I will," said the boy. Then, just as he was about to ask if he'd ever see the fish again, the fish disappeared under the water and, for a few seconds, everything under the water lit up, turning all the vibrant colors of a sunset. And then, just as quickly as it had come to life, the water went dark and still again, leaving the boy there in his boat staring at his hand, at the mark left there by the strange and beautiful talking fish.

"Is that it?"

"That's it. Goodnight, Doug. I love you. You know that, right?"

"I know that."

"Good."

"That story was about today, wasn't it? About me getting my hand cutted."

"Sort of."

"So you think I'm a warrior?"

"I *know* you're a warrior."

KAY NOTICED A light on in the Scamp. Maybe Douglas had come home. But when had it gotten dark? It seemed like only minutes ago the sun was out. The door to the Scamp was open just a bit, so Kay gave a little knock in case Douglas was in there. When she called his name and there was no response, the silence unnerved her for some reason. And the light seeping out through the cracked door seemed to be shaking. Like someone was moving around inside. "Hello? Is someone in there?" Again, there was no response. She opened the door a little more and peered in. The first thing she noticed was the size and number of them. There had to have been at least a hundred of them, all the size of silver dollars. The gypsy moths were blanketing the ceiling light, swarming like they were trying to devour the thing. She'd have to have a word with Douglas about turning that damn light off before he left for work in the mornings.

Her first instinct was to grab a hand towel and swat at them, but she knew from experience it would be useless. There was a pull chain on the light, and when she reached for it, a few of the moths alighted onto her hand. She pulled her hand away from the gray, feather-like mass and sat down on the bench seat. There were two of them crawling around the back of her hand now, looking for something to eat no doubt and probably disappointed that her liver spots were just that: spots. They were soft, beautiful things though.

Destructive beasts, maybe, but gorgeous nonetheless. Kay had always liked moths, felt they'd gotten a bad rap when compared to butterflies. It didn't seem fair that they were always the ugly cousin. Humans liked big, colorful things. But the moth was like a steppe covered in snow. Or a lake holding a dull cup of fog.

Kay held her hand up to her face, and one of the moths flitted back toward what was left of the light. The remaining moth was still except for the rabbit ears on its head slowly swiveling from side to side. Kay thought of the jars filled with soapy water she'd set out last summer to lure the caterpillars, drowning them before metamorphosis could occur. It had to be done; she understood that. But what she held now seemed like a gray explosion in her hand and suddenly Kay felt herself close to tears.

"You have to tell him."

She could hear Norm as clearly as if he were sitting there beside her. She knew the moth wasn't her husband, but, even so, she spoke to it.

"I know. I will."

She wiped away a tear and, when she did, the moth left her hand, disappearing into the undulating furry ball that the light had become. She sat in silence for a bit, waiting for her husband to speak again. When he didn't, she picked up Douglas's sketchbook from the table and pulled on the chain throwing the Scamp into darkness.

LATER, AS KAY sat watching another episode of *Murder She Wrote* with a Manhattan bigger than the city it was named after, the fact that Norm never told her about the poetry seemed like a betrayal of sorts, keeping that part of himself hidden from her. But there was something else bothering Kay. The thought was there, half-formed and hazy, flitting about the corners of her mind like the gypsy moths earlier. And, like the light pushing its way through the gathering bodies, the thought, shaky as it was, eventually made its way through. *What secrets did Kay have? What secrets were hers?* And the answer to that, the absolute soul-toppling answer to that seemed to beat quietly inside her as she fell asleep yet again on the couch:

None.

CHAPTER FIFTEEN
Douglas

DOUGLAS WAS PUTTING the shovel and pickaxe back in the shed, about to go inside for lunch, when he saw his mother making her way slowly down the steps. She was making a big show of it, smiling broadly like a movie star descending some grand staircase. "They're beautiful," she said, once she reached the bottom. "Really."

"Better late than never, I guess."

"Late? Why would you say that?"

"Never mind."

He'd shored them up using 4 X 6's and rebar pounded into the dirt so they wouldn't crumble in the summer rains and laid rocks on top so they wouldn't puddle. And he'd been sure to make them snake down the hill so they wouldn't be too steep for his mom. Douglas liked them, though it was a bitter-sweet kind of like. He could almost see Norm trudging up the steps, his fishing rod in hand, a beating heart still in his chest.

"Is there something you want to tell me, honey?"

"I don't know. Is there something *you* want to tell me?"

His mother studied him a moment. "Why don't you go first. Mine can wait."

"You sure you won't forget?" Douglas walked over to one of the steps, avoiding his mother's gaze, and kicked at the rebar.

"You know, don't you?"

"Shawna and I are pretty close, Mom. You can't blame her for telling me."

"No. No, I don't. Not at all."

Douglas watched as his mom walked out on the dock. She shuffled when she walked now. Or was beginning to. And her shoulders were rounding out, hunching over. It was like she was slowly disappearing right before his eyes. When he sat down next to her on the bench, her eyes were wet and large as she looked out toward the island. She seemed so incredibly vulnerable and scared. Just like that night his dad died. It was something Douglas hoped he'd never have to see again.

"I'm not going to tell you I'm pregnant every day." He waited for a response, but his mom only nodded, obviously not listening to him. "Okay, maybe I will."

"You will what now, honey?"

"Tell you I'm pregnant every day."

"Why on earth would you do something like that?"

Douglas reached over, squeezed her hand. When

he went to pull away, though, she held onto it. "I saw something once about a woman whose mother had Alzheimer's, and every day the daughter would tell her mom she was pregnant. Each time the mom would get all excited and super happy. It was supposed to be one of those feel-good stories they have on the news."

She pulled her hand away. "You have to promise you'll never do that to me."

"Well, seeing as I can't get pregnant..."

"You know what I mean, Douglas. I'm serious now. Promise me. Promise me you'll never treat me like a... like an imbecile. I'd rather be dead."

"Okay, I promise. I get it."

She looked at him, the fear seeming to ebb some, then back out at the island. "Can I ask why you keep staring at the island?"

She reached for his hand again. "I don't know. It's pretty?"

"It's not that pretty."

"No, I suppose not."

"You're going to be okay."

"Not really."

"No, I guess not."

"I'm scared, Douglas. Is it okay to tell you that?"

"Yeah, it's okay. I am, too."

"Just treat me with respect. That's all I ask."

"So *not* like when you had all your faculties still intact."

"Very funny."

They were quiet for a bit, the wind picking up on the lake, setting little ripples in motion across the surface. It always reminded Douglas of a miniature-sized typhoon the way the water rocked the dock, leaving a root-beer colored foam along the bank.

"Your turn," his mother said after a bit.

"My turn what?"

"You were going to tell me something about the steps."

"I guess it couldn't hurt."

"What does that mean?"

"Well, it's not like you're going to remember anyway, right?" He gave her a gentle nudge with his shoulder. "Too soon?"

"Just tell me before I die of old age."

Douglas found himself looking out at the island now, too, like maybe the answers to both their problems were hiding out there among the cattails. "Dad asked me to build them."

"The steps? When?"

"A few weeks before..."

"Oh, Douglas honey."

"Yeah. Oh, Douglas honey."

"And you think that had something to do with why your father had a heart attack?"

"Well, he *did* ask me to put them in. And I just kept putting it off like I do everything. And he did die walking back up to the house. So, yeah, I kind of totally think it's my fault."

His mom shook her head and sighed. "Your father's death was no more your fault than it was mine for cooking him all those steaks over the years. And he'd been muttering about putting in those damn steps for years, along with about a dozen or so other projects he was never going to get around to. If he wanted them built so badly, he could've done it himself a long time ago rather than trying to pass it off on you."

"Still."

"Still nothing. I don't want you walking around with that mess inside you. You hear me? It's not... Well, it's just not accurate."

Douglas felt the fist his throat had turned into loosen a touch. "I don't know about that, but thanks for saying it anyway."

"Well, it's true. And I know Norm would tell you the same thing if he could. It wasn't your fault, Douglas. It wasn't anybody's fault. That man's heart was older and more banged up than any of those clunkers down at the shop."

Douglas could hear her and knew she meant every word, but he also knew she could tell him the same thing every day for the rest of his life and it still wouldn't be enough to kill the guilt he felt. He would forever be the one bringing that particular hammer down on himself. This much he knew for certain.

"Thanks, Mom. Maybe you're right."

"There's no maybe about it. It's true. I say so."

Douglas shook his head, stood up, and held out his hand to her. "At least I had nothing to do with your Alzheimer's. There's that anyway."

His mother coughed loudly and looked down at her feet. "Well, let's not get too carried away."

"You're really not funny."

His mother rose from the bench, slid her arm through his. "I guess that makes two of us then."

———

SHE HAD INSISTED on going to the transfer station with him, said she needed to get out of the house for a bit even if it was just down to the dump. As they drove, Douglas spotted a family of deer through the jack pines and found himself wondering if animals got Alzheimer's, too.

"How would you know if a deer had Alzheimer's?"

His mother kept staring out the window, not bothering to turn her head when she answered him. "I don't know. How?"

"There isn't a punchline or anything, Mom. I'm seriously asking."

"Oh," she said, sounding a little disappointed. "I don't think animals get sick like that, honey. It's probably just a human thing."

"Like serial killers?"

"I suppose."

She sounded tired. Or maybe she sounded like an adult, and here he was bothering her with stupid questions like a child. Probably the latter, he realized, but still he wasn't able to let it go.

"I mean, you wouldn't be able to tell if a deer, or any other animal, lost their memory. How would their behavior change? How much is just instinct? Or can you lose instinct, too?"

"I hope we don't see anyone there. I'm not in the mood to talk to people."

Douglas took the hint, dropped it. "Seriously? You're always in the mood to talk."

"You sound like your father."

Douglas remembered his dad saying something about how conversation, if done right, could be like a good meal but that most people were just pigs. Not that his mom was like that. Douglas just liked to tease her about it from time to time.

The transfer station turned out to be practically empty. After Douglas had unloaded the trunk of the week's garbage and recycling, he was planning on driving back home when his mother asked if they could make a little detour.

"I was thinking we could stop at that new coffee shop. Alma told me I should try one of those coffee mochas."

"Café mochas."

"Isn't that what I said?"

Douglas hadn't spoken to Jenna since his last visit. Not because he hadn't wanted to, but more out of embarrassment. Still, he could think of no plausible excuse for avoiding the stop.

"They're not cheap, you know."

"The coffee? They can't be that much. Besides, I think I'm allowed to splurge a little, considering."

Douglas smiled at her. "You're really going to milk this for all it's worth, aren't you?"

"I'm sure I don't know what you're talking about."

When they got there, Jenna was behind the counter, her back to them, cleaning something in the sink. Douglas had thought of telling his mother about her, that he'd been seeing her, but for some reason, he didn't. Mainly, he supposed, because he wasn't quite sure how to label what they were yet. Douglas watched as his mom took in the artwork on the walls. With her hand on her chin she could have just as easily been trying to decide which can of soup to buy down at Snow's. But, then, that's probably what Douglas looked like, too, when looking at paintings.

"I don't know why exactly, but I really like this one."

She had stopped in front of a large painting of a red loon lying in the road with a broken neck, black blood bleeding out and around the edges of the frame. Douglas's loon, more or less, though Jenna's was definitely more disturbing. When Douglas peered down at the white card taped to the wall, it read simply "Douglas O'Brien." He was waiting for his mother to notice, but she seemed transfixed by the painting. More so, he noted with a slight pang, than she'd ever seemed to be when looking at his own drawings.

"I think I've seen this somewhere before."

"Yeah. On a road."

"I mean in another painting, smartass."

It was clear she'd been peeking at his sketchbook, and Douglas was about to call her on it when Jenna walked up behind them.

"Hi." Jenna stood there looking first at Douglas, and then at Kay, waiting, it seemed, for Douglas to make the next move. She was smiling coyly, though, as if his discomfort were the source of infinite joy to her.

"Hello," his mother said. "I think I'd like a *café* mocha, please. Do you have any of those?"

"I do have those. What size would you like?"

"I think a small would be just fine."

"A small it is. And for you, sir?"

"Mom, this is Jenna. Jenna, this is my mom."

His mother's face lit up as she took the girl in, making it obvious, to Douglas anyway, that she deemed Jenna somewhat out of his league. "Oh, is this the new friend you've been spending so much time with?"

"Mom."

"I'll take that as a yes." She held her hand out and the two shook hands. "I'm Catherine. But everybody calls me Kay."

"Which do you prefer?"

"You know, I don't think anyone's ever asked me that."

"People call me Jen all the time and it drives me nuts. That's the only reason I ask."

"That makes sense. I'd like Jenna better, too, I think."

There was an awkward silence and Douglas could tell his mother had forgotten the question entirely. "Mom."

"What?"

"Kay or Catherine?"

"Oh, right. Why don't you just call me Kay like everyone

else. But you know what's funny? Now that I think about it, I don't think I really like either name."

"You could always change it."

"Oh, that would be too silly at my age. And what on earth would I change it to?"

"Fred," Douglas muttered, which only elicited frowns from both women.

"All I'm saying is that you could. Probably a big hassle, though, and I think Kay is pretty cool as is."

"Cool? Oh, I don't know about that."

"Sure it is. I don't know anyone called Kay. Or Catherine for that matter."

"That's probably because it's a name from a time long past. My mother named me after the saint, the one they tortured."

"Really?" Douglas said. "I never knew that."

"Saint Catherine of the Wheel."

"She's the patron saint of wheels?"

"No, they tortured her on some kind of spiked wheel. When that didn't work, they cut her head off and milk poured out."

"Jesus."

"Exactly."

"See," Jenna said, "I told you it was a cool name."

Douglas was starting to feel invisible the way the two were getting on. He wondered if she'd be so enamored with Jenna if she knew what she used to do for a living. Possibly. He never knew with his mother. If there ever was a living contradiction, his mom was it. "So I really like the new painting and all, but, if I'm being honest, I don't think it looks all that much like me."

"Oh, I don't know," Jenna said, moving to his side. "I can definitely see a resemblance."

"You painted these? Wow, I'm impressed."

"Thank you."

"I don't know if I'd want them hanging in my living room, but I think they're great. Is that okay to say?"

Jenna smiled at her. "It's completely okay to say. I admire tons of paintings that I wouldn't necessarily want hanging in my home."

"Oh, good, I thought I might have offended you."

"The only thing that offends me is when people bash art for no real reason. I mean, even if you don't like something, somebody made an effort to make something meaningful. Most people who trash things haven't ever even tried. They don't understand what it's like to risk failing." Jenna adjusted her apron, dusted off some grounds along the front. "I'm sorry. I didn't mean to give a speech."

Kay laughed. "If that's a speech then I'm a regular politician. Isn't that right, Douglas? Your old mother likes to talk, doesn't she?"

"I never noticed."

"Whatever. I haven't gone over to the other side just yet." Jenna gave them both a quizzical look and before Douglas could stop her, his mother began to explain. "I've been diagnosed with Alzheimer's. Which is fine, but chances are in a few months I won't remember who you are. So don't take it personally or anything is what I'm trying to say."

"I'm so sorry. I had no idea. Douglas, you didn't--"

"I only just found out."

"Oh. Well, I'm still sorry. That must be scary."

"I don't know. It might be fun. I was never all there to begin with anyway, was I, Douglas?"

"Mom."

"Oh, settle down. She can handle it, can't you?"

"I can. And, yeah, settle down."

With that, Jenna left to get their coffees though Douglas never did get a chance to tell her his order. She'd no doubt return with some fancy concoction that looked and tasted nothing like coffee but that Douglas would end up liking despite himself. They sat at the window overlooking the street, the same spot he'd sat at when he first came there with Shawna. It seemed so long ago now, like multiple years had somehow been stuffed inside this last one. A turducken year.

"I like her," his mother said, staring out the window.

"I can see that."

"And she's pretty, too."

"She is. Very."

"For a while there your father and I weren't sure if--"

"Don't. I know."

"Not that it would matter."

"Stop."

"Okay."

Douglas flipped through the local paper, *The Daily Globe*, while his mom did her best to keep quiet. He could tell she was excited because she kept fidgeting with her hands, rubbing at the veins. Douglas, trying to distract himself, flipped to the police blotter in the back of the paper. It was something he and Marty liked to do during their lunch breaks.

- 8:46 a.m. -A Minocqua man reported that his girlfriend threatened to ruin his boat and damage his new snowmobile.

- 12:37 p.m. -A Mercer resident reported that the neighbor's pig was out and rooting through garbage. The pig was walked home and put back in its yard.

- 6:42 p.m. –Dog Attack at Sweetheart Lake- Police responded to a report of a dog running loose and attacking a pair of swans. The officer cited a resident for the loose dog. The swans refused medical treatment and left the area, according to police records.

- 2:30 a.m. -Three men driving a Buick sedan crashed into a tree after leaving Lake of the Torches Casino early Sunday morning. One of the men is said to have died at the scene. The other two are in stable condition at Mercer Hospital. Alcohol is believed to have been involved.

Douglas was about to hand the paper to his mother when an article on the opposite page caught his eye.

Loon Burning Update

Locals in Mercer, who are now openly referring to the arsonist as "The Loonadick," haven't been too happy about the lack of progress in finding the culprit who destroyed their town's beloved wooden mascot. But police now say they are following up on an important lead and are confident it will result in an arrest (or arrests) soon.

"One small café mocha with whipped cream. I hope the whipped cream is okay."

"Oh, I think whipped cream is always okay, don't you?"

"I do, indeed. And here's one fuchsia gluten-free pineapple-infused Americano latte decaf soy with cinnamon. No whipped cream."

Douglas forced a smile as he took the to-go cup from her.

"Aren't you going to try it?"

"Mine's delicious," Kay said, taking another sip. "I usually just drink instant."

"Well, we're going to have to do something about that. Douglas?"

Douglas took a sip and grimaced dramatically.

"Oh, it can't be that bad now," his mom said, looking like she wanted to backhand him one.

"It's just regular old black coffee. Thank you."

"I know what you like."

A smile passed between them, and Douglas felt his

heart swelling, like multiple hearts had been stuffed inside his one heart. A turducken heart.

Later, as they were driving back home, his mom, out of nowhere, said, "They don't fear people anymore."

"Who doesn't fear people?"

"Your question. About the deer. That's how you can tell."

He looked over at her, at the childlike smile she wore, and, not for the first time, thought maybe his mother was the wisest person on Earth.

CHAPTER SIXTEEN
Shawna

THERE'D BEEN A town meeting where people got to vote on whether the old Loon should be salvaged somehow, rebuilt, or if they should build something new. Overwhelmingly, people had voted for a new, and, of course, bigger Loon. As a result, a small crowd had gathered to watch the giant wooden bird be diced up into firewood. Shawna had wondered if people would be sad, but the overall atmosphere was like a county fair, children chasing one another with their hands over their ears while their parents chatted. Shawna, unsure of how it would affect her, found she felt nothing. Or, at the very least, felt the perverse thrill of a voyeur. When there was a break in the butchering, random parts of the old bird being tossed into a pickup, Elmer finally responded to her question.

"No."

"Why not?"

"Because it isn't right."

"Since when did you become all moral."

"You can just go around doing things like that to people who've wronged you."

"Wronged me? He was friends with my step-dad. He's the Treaty Beer guy. He tried to steal Seven. I'm tired of nothing bad ever happening to him because the people he's messing with are nice and decent."

"You *are* decent."

"Well, I guess I'm going through some changes then because I've come to the conclusion that decency is overrated."

"You'll regret it if you go through with it. And you'll probably end up going to jail, too."

Shawna nodded toward what was left of the toppled Loon. "Yeah? You think so?"

"Don't get cocky. Just because you haven't been caught doesn't mean they won't figure it out eventually."

"Once they run those DNA tests?"

"I'm telling you, Shawna. Don't. Just don't. Think about vet school. Think about us leaving here next year. Don't let somebody like him get in the way of that. You're better than that."

"Maybe I'm not."

"Fuck that. You're a hundred-foot loon and he's a...a frog or whatever it is loons eat."

"They eat frogs. And fish and leeches, I think."

"See, you know that because you're a nerd and are supposed to go to school with other nerds who love animals. He's just a little white frog. Forget about him."

The chainsaws started up again, making conversation impossible. Which was fine with Shawna since, apparently, Elmer wasn't about to help her exact her revenge on Peyton Crane. As she watched the city workers cut through a good-sized blackened chunk of the Loon's left wing, she knew Elmer was right. He usually was. And while that infuriated her, it had also stopped her from doing about 36 incredibly stupid things since her mom died. This latest idea no doubt topping the list.

SOME BOYS NEED to be forced into manhood.

Seven didn't seem interested in going out, so Shawna busied herself by digging the hoof pick into the grooves of Seven's hooves, trying to dislodge anything that might have worked itself in. Seven had been acting lethargic ever since she'd brought him back home. His coat, too, had lost some of its usual sheen. Shawna hoped a thorough grooming might cheer him up.

The sun can warm, but it can also decay.

Her mother's voice accompanied the cleaning, there in the background like a TV left on. Bits and pieces came through, some that made sense to Shawna and others that didn't. When she finished with the hooves, Shawna grabbed the metal curry comb and began to gently move it in circles along Seven's coat. She did this slowly, lovingly, as she knew Seven's skin was sometimes sensitive to the metal. Normally, at some point when using the comb, he would bristle or whinny, annoyed and irritated. But there was none of that today. Another thing that was starting to worry Shawna.

You will have to summon every breath of light inside you to bring about a darkness.

Before Shawna started brushing Seven's head and mane with his body brush, she placed her head against him and smelled his coat. There was nothing foul or sickly in the smell. He simply smelled like Seven, the same as the inside of her car and all her clothes had since she'd gotten him. It was her favorite smell in the world. Shawna stopped to clean out the brush, which had become nearly full with all the debris loosened by the curry comb, and as she did, she spoke softly to Seven.

"You'll come to Madison with us, so don't worry about that. We'll find someplace with a big backyard, and I'll take you out for walks whenever I can. I won't lie; it won't be as nice as here. But at least we'll still be together. You'll just have to trust me that things will work out."

Shawna ran the brush along his withers, then his back and side and belly and croup, ending up along his hind legs, all the while giving the brush little flicks so that the dirt flew free of his coat.

We are always, at all times, afraid. This is awareness. This is being alive.

Shawna saved the tail for last, knowing it was full of tangles from not having been properly combed in some time. She worked her fingers through the hair first, saving the comb for later so as not to rip any clumps of hair out.

"Almost done, sexy boy. Then maybe you'll let me take you for a quick run?"

But instead of stamping his feet like he usually did when Shawna mentioned taking him out, Seven slowly and painstakingly lay himself down on the ground. Something he had never done during grooming.

"Okay, I guess we're done with grooming then."

It was clear to Shawna that something was wrong, though. She threw a blanket over Seven and kissed his nose. His breathing was suddenly labored. Shallow. Even his eyelids seemed to be having trouble staying open. What the hell was happening?

"I'm calling Judy, okay? I'll be right back. I promise."

Shawna ran inside and phoned the local vet. When there was no answer, she left a hurried message asking her to come as soon as possible. Judy Farrell was something of a hero to Shawna. She was both a strong *and* happy woman. A rarity in life, as far as Shawna had seen. And she could almost always tell what was wrong with an animal, or so it seemed to Shawna, just by looking at them or running a hand under their belly.

Back outside, Shawna tried to get Seven to drink a little water, but he was having none of it. It was like he'd been hit with a tranquilizer dart, all his energy sapped instantly. She tried telling herself that he just needed some sleep and then he'd be fine, but everything she was seeing was telling her differently.

She sat down in the dirt beside Seven, stroking his forelock. "You're the most handsome boy in the world. You know that, right?"

She couldn't be sure, but there looked to be swelling around his eyes. And his throat, too, seemed puffed up now. She was about to run inside to call Judy again when she spotted the petals in the dirt. She hadn't noticed them before because they were mixed in with loose bits of hay. She picked one up, recognizing it straightaway as foxglove because her naan had made sure to pull all the ones she'd planted around the house when they'd gotten Seven. Shawna also remembered the flower because the name had never made any sense to her. How did this tube-like thing with paw prints on the inside resemble a fox's glove? Shawna soon found others mixed in with the hay, little bits and pieces of purple everywhere, almost like someone had been hand-feeding them to Seven.

"Baby, what did you eat? Who gave this to you?"

She would go inside and call the vet again. Surely she could give him something, some sort of antidote, and Seven would eventually recover. She started to get up, but Seven started paddling his legs around in the dirt. His eyes were swollen into slits now.

I'll take care of him, Shawna. I promise.

"No," Shawna said out loud and then she couldn't stop saying it as Seven's throat began to twitch. He then released his bowels into the dirt, his legs straining out like they were trying to separate themselves from his body, like he was being electrocuted, and seconds later her best friend was gone.

By the time Judy showed up the next morning, Shawna had covered Seven's body with all of his favorite blankets. Shawna, too, felt covered in blankets, weighted down. It was like a big hand was pressing down on her so that all she wanted to do was remain still. But Shawna had learned a trick long ago, a way to create a spark which then turned to flame and burned away the fog. It was called anger.

"I can't be sure unless I run some tests, but it looks to me like your suspicions are accurate. If somebody had interlaced a significant amount of foxglove with Seven's feed, then it wouldn't take long for a chronic seizure like this to occur. Especially if they'd been doing it over a couple of days. I know it won't give you much comfort right now to hear this, but there wasn't much you could have done to save him. I hate to ask you this right now, but do you have any guesses as to who might have done something like this?"

"No," Shawna lied.

She wanted to build a pyre out of wood and set Seven's body adrift on the lake before setting him on fire much in the same way she had the town loon. It was something she wanted done with her own body when her time came; there was something simple and complete and beautiful in it. But, Judy was quick to point out, it was, unfortunately, illegal. "And not so great for the environment either, I might add." Burying Seven wasn't an option either, apparently. In the end, Judy made arrangements with a rendering plant that would pick Seven up the following day, the idea of which seemed monumentally disrespectful to Shawna. How could something mean so much to someone and then just be carted off like an old couch?

People came and went for the rest of the day. Douglas and his mom kept checking up on Shawna, and, at some point in the afternoon, Kay had brought over two BLTs and 3 cans of root beer. All of which Shawna devoured, alone, sitting beside the mound of blankets. She peeked once under the covers and saw a white film had covered Seven's still-open eyes, making him look like a giant dead fish. She had never seen her mother's death face because she was left without one. It was one of those things which, when piled on top of the magnitude of horrific, was maybe silly to resent. But Shawna always had. She was denied not being able to kiss her mother's cold face goodbye. Had the monster thought about that for even a second? No. To do so would have made him human. Which he wasn't. So Shawna did it now. She lifted the blanket, closed Seven's eyelids, and pressed her face against the side of his head and kissed him.

Douglas at some point brought her coffee and a bag of potato chips and another blanket. Words were spoken, but Shawna mostly did a lot of nodding and shaking of her head. Seven had been the suit of armor she wore after her Mom died, and now she was naked, retreating once again deep inside herself, a rage slowly weaving what would soon clothe her. Her naan came out at twilight and burned some sage over Seven's body while softly singing an Ojibwa prayer over him. By the time she finished, tears were spilling down her wrinkled cheeks. When she went inside for the night, Shawna rested a hand on the mound of blankets. "Did you see that? You made a stone bleed. That's how incredible you are."

She thought about calling Elmer but just couldn't bring

herself to do it. She knew he'd stay by her side, wrap her up in his big arms and keep quiet when she needed quiet. He was built for mourning; she realized that now. Maybe it was just living he wasn't built for. She decided to take the pen down the next day, donate or burn all of Seven's things, maybe plant a garden of foxglove in the place he'd died.

When it got too dark to see, Douglas brought out a Coleman lantern for her. "You want me to build you a fire? I wouldn't mind at all." Shawna shook her head. "It'll get cold." She patted the sleeping bag she'd brought out. "Can I sit with you for a while then?" Shawna looked at him steadily for a moment, and he understood like she knew he would. "Okay, got it. If you change your mind, just come knock on my window." Nod, nod. "Goodnight, then. I'm sorry, Shawna."

How much more will you let them take from us?

Shawna waited, curled up beside Seven in her sleeping bag, for as long as she could, but it was like her sleeping bag was full of mosquitoes. At some point, almost like she was sleepwalking, she went into the garage and pulled out her headlamp and spear and her old tackle box. Then she got into her car and, without turning on the headlights, slowly drove off down the road.

CHAPTER SEVENTEEN
Douglas

DOUGLAS DIDN'T NEED to be at the shop that day, but he decided to stop in and see Marty. Someone in the bar the other night was shooting their mouth off about a sweet spot nobody knew about behind the church. Which was probably true, as Douglas doubted the new priest did much fishing.

"I don't know," Marty said, taking a break from doing a whole lot of nothing as far as Douglas could see. "Wasn't Jesus all about loaves and fishes? Maybe it's packed full of fish."

"Loaves? Where do you get this stuff from? I suppose you think the lake is filled with Wonder Bread, too." Douglas set two lawn chairs out for them on the sidewalk. "You ever tried bacon for bait? I bet that'd work."

"Sure. We used to use hot dogs when I was a kid."

"Cooked?"

"Yeah, with ketchup and onions and sauerkraut. No, not cooked, you moron."

Douglas was about to tell Marty about the silver box his mom had found, about the poems, when a police car pulled into the lot.

"Jesus, what'd you do now? Burn down a giant wooden swan somewhere?"

"Shut up, Marty."

Douglas had regretted telling Marty about the loon incident, but he'd needed to tell someone. It wasn't every day, after all, that he committed a felony. And while he could have chosen a better confidant, Marty, as far as he knew, had kept his mouth shut about it.

"Afternoon, boys."

Chris Turner had graduated a few years ahead of them, but they'd both heard the stories about how he liked to bully the freshmen. Pretty much nobody liked Chris Turner. And, to make things worse, once he became a cop, the jerk had started demanding that people call him Christopher, rather than Chris, which is what he'd always gone by in high school.

"Hey, Chris. Heard you broke up Little Tyler's party the other night at, like, 10:30. Things that slow for you guys?"

Officer Christopher glared at Marty briefly before directing his answer to Douglas. It was always like this. Marty was a step above a cockroach in his eyes because he wasn't the owner. Even Mercer had a kind of caste system. "We had numerous complaints from neighbors. They knew better."

"So what brings you in?" Douglas said, all polite like he was talking to somebody's grandmother. It was something he'd picked up from his dad. "She giving you trouble again?"

The police and fire department had a contract with a bigger shop, A-1 Mechanics, on the outskirts of town but Norm had always taken care of the local cops if they had something small that needed doing. And, of course, they also wanted it kept off the books.

"Something's not right. If I get her up past sixty, it starts making this sound."

"What kind of sound is it?" Marty said, sounding deadly serious though Douglas knew otherwise. "It'll help us out if you could, you know, sort of reenact it for us."

"It's like this whirring sound. *Whirrrrrrr.*"

"Well, that would definitely be a whirring sound, Chris. Anything else you can tell us? You know, to narrow down the suspects."

"Well, it tends to happen on Wednesdays and Thursdays for some reason."

"Wednesdays and Thursdays, Douglas. You thinking what I'm thinking?"

"We'll get it up on the lift and take a look," Douglas said, trying his best to keep a straight face. "Just give us a few minutes."

"Fine by me. Maybe I'll head down to that new coffee shop, see this new owner people are talking about."

"She's an artist. Isn't that right, Douglas?"

"I'm sure Officer Christopher here would prefer it if we

figure out what's wrong with his ride rather than sit here and gossip."

"Speaking of gossip, we found some arrowheads stuck in the goddamn loon. Don't go talking about that now; it's police business. But I was thinking about that Burning Men Festival all those artist types go to. Maybe this coffee shop owner is one of them. I mean nobody ever set the Loon on fire before, and now here she is moving into town only recently, right?"

"Wow," Marty said, taking the keys from him. "I never would have thought of that. But, then again, that's probably why I'm not a cop."

"That's *definitely* why you aren't a cop."

Douglas powered up the lift. "She's not like that. She's a decent person."

"Well, they're all decent. Before they're not. I guess I'll find out soon enough for myself."

Once Officer Christopher had left, Marty drove the cruiser onto the lift. When he got out, he was smiling, shaking his head. "Mercer's finest, ladies and gentlemen."

"He's alright."

"He's alright? He's sure as shit a long way away from alright." When Douglas didn't respond, Marty added, "All I know is if that were my girl, I'd at least warn her a storm of dickhead was headed her way."

"She's not my girl, but she can handle herself. I'd be more worried about him."

"Fine. But you mind telling me why you're always in

such a hurry to help him? We both know we've got other shit needs getting done."

"It's just good business. That's all."

"You sound like someone trying to do an impersonation of Norm."

"Well, I guess I kind of *am* an impersonation of Norm seeing as I'm his son. Can we just get this over with, please?"

"Jeez, okay. What's eating you? You get that coffee woman pregnant or something?"

"The cruiser, Marty."

"You got the cruiser pregnant? Wow, it's more serious than I thought."

Douglas ignored him and busied himself running a few checks though he already knew it was a fuel line issue. Marty, in a rare feat, managed to be quiet for nearly an entire fifteen minutes before breaking the silence.

"So are you worried Officer Chris suspects something? About the loon, I mean."

"No, but let's not give him any reason to."

"Easier said than done. That guy's suspicious of puddles."

"It'll be fine. They probably think it was just a couple of drunk teenagers."

"Uh, it basically *was* a couple of drunk teenagers." Marty shined a light up through the bowels of the engine. "Anyway, it's just not like you, man. You don't do stuff like that."

"Well, maybe I do now."

"Now? So, like, you're going to burn shit down on the regular now?"

"Maybe."

"Yeah, Kay would just love that." Marty paused, then added, "She doing alright now?"

"You saw her that night. You think she's doing alright?"

"I don't know. I just figured she had one too many. Plus, her being old, you know. Their brains must be tired by that age. So they, you know, slip sometimes."

"Slip?"

Marty nodded. "Sure. Happens all the time."

Douglas was about to tell him the news since Marty was going to find out one way or another eventually, but Officer Wonderful came back.

"Any verdict yet?"

"Guilty," Marty said and shined the light in his face. "On all counts."

Douglas hurried over, lowered Marty's hand. "I haven't spotted anything out of the ordinary yet, but I'll go ahead and flush out your fuel line just in case."

"And how long will that take?"

"Fifteen, maybe twenty, minutes."

"Better make it fifteen. Hey, this coffee she made is like candy. You should get yourself one sometime."

"So the town arsonist made a good cup of Joe, huh," Marty said. "Good to know."

"Oh, she's no arsonist. Maybe a druggie, but no

arsonist. I don't know how she expects to run a business with all that crap hanging on the walls."

"I like them," Douglas said quietly.

"Me, too," Marty said, "though I haven't seen them yet."

"Whatever," Officer Christopher said, still not bothering to look at Marty. "Nice gal, though. And pretty, too. Even with that hair of hers."

"So who's next on your list of suspects then? Maybe you think Douglas and I torched the bird. Maybe there's nothing really wrong with your car at all."

"Well, did you?"

"I did not, Officer. But I can't speak for my esteemed colleague here."

Douglas shot Marty a look. "I'm sure he'd much rather we finish the job. How about we focus on that?"

"I believe they refer to that as evasion."

"I didn't burn down the fucking Loon, okay? Satisfied?"

"Uh, yeah, totally satisfied. How about you, Officer?"

"You two are something else. That's all I know."

Marty laughed. "Norm always said that, too. And then he'd say *And when I figure out what, I'll let you know.*"

Officer Christopher didn't so much as grin at this, which probably shouldn't have surprised anybody. The guy's idea of funny probably had something to do with torturing small rodents. Once they'd finished with the cruiser and Officer Christopher was safely on his way, Douglas, in a voice trembling with anger, said, "What in the hell was that all about?"

Marty was at the sink, lathering on the *Go-Jo*. "Yeah, sorry about that. I didn't expect you to react all weird like that."

"It's a felony, Marty. So, yeah, I was a little nervous about it, especially around that psychopath."

"I just thought it might throw him off. Like reverse psychology and all that."

"Well, it didn't. If anything, the moron probably thinks I did it now."

"Probably thinks you murdered someone, too. I mean the way you were acting and everything. I mean, Jesus."

"Marty."

"Yeah?"

"Shut it."

"Right."

BY THE TIME Douglas got to the bar, Marty was already three well whiskeys deep, not to mention the handful of Leineys he'd probably had in his car beforehand. When Douglas sat down across from him, Marty, a faint slur already going, said, "Don't you have a shoe that needs gazing at?"

"I see you're at the witty stage already."

"So what brings you down here anyway? Jenna leave you already?"

"I was hoping Shawna might be here."

"She hates this place."

"Just thought she might. You not hear about Seven?"

"No. What?"

"Somebody poisoned him."

"Seriously? With what?"

"Foxglove. They think so anyway."

"Fox what? Sounds like a perfume."

"It's a flower, dumbass. Apparently, it's poisonous if you eat enough."

"What kind of asshole would do something like that? Does she know?"

"She's not saying much."

"What a wonderful world."

The bar was surprisingly full considering it was past ten. Peyton Crane was there, unusually quiet for once, possibly exhausted from spouting off his usual bullshit to those eager to hear anything other than their own miserable thoughts.

"Are you going to go look for her?"

"She probably went to see Elmer is my guess."

"Yeah, nothing like death to get the old juices flowing."

"Ease up, Marty."

"What? It's true. Funerals are like aphrodisiacs for..." Marty stopped himself, catching the look Douglas was giving him. "Right, okay. But you get my point."

"Sure."

There was some laughter at the bar, only it sounded to Douglas more like a long, cackling fuck-you.

"What are they so worked up about?"

"Something about Indians being worse than Mexicans because at least Mexicans can cook decent food."

"I thought you'd be all over that."

"Nah, I actually like Mexicans."

"How noble of you."

"The priest was in here earlier. You just missed him."

"That's a shame. Was he wearing his Birkenstocks?"

"He was. Sat at the end of the bar, near the door. I think he likes having an escape route."

"Can't blame him. Not with these assholes here every night."

"They tried to get him into a debate, something about Indians going to hell for being heathens, but he wouldn't bite. He just kept telling them to come visit him in his office or come to Bible study class."

"I'm sure that went over well."

"The usual sniggering."

"But not you?"

"No."

"Are you ill?"

"Funny."

"So?"

"So, nothing. I guess I'm just tired of it." Marty paused, stared down into his drink. "It's like Shawna and her people have always been here, you know. And, like, we're the tourists."

"You're just realizing this now?"

"No. But I don't really care either. Someday someone

else will be sitting here drinking cheap whiskey and talking shit about white people. It's kind of just how things work."

"You had me worried there for a second. I thought maybe you felt guilty or something."

Marty shook his head, then, lowering his voice, "Do you think you'll ever leave here? I mean, is this it?"

"You mean move somewhere? Why? Do *you* want to move somewhere?"

"No, I'm just becoming convinced nobody ever really gets out of here. Like the idea of leaving is just all Hollywood-type thinking."

"People leave all the time, Marty. Remember Sharon?"

"She got married and moved to Chicago with that dentist guy. That's one, I guess."

"You're just drunk. People leave all the time. Why don't you? It might be good for you."

"Because I like it here. That's the difference between you and me. And maybe there's nowhere to go really. Maybe it's all just the same shit more or less. Look at Jenna. She *chose* to move here. That has to say something."

"Look at those guys." Douglas nodded to the bar, at Peyton Crane who was stooped over so low at this point that his forehead was only inches from the bar. "Bunch of Cro-Magnon turd balls."

"There's a lot of good people here, too. You know that. Your mom being one of them."

Douglas nodded. His mom. She was a saint compared to most people. "I guess we both got lucky in that department."

"I guess we did."

By the time Douglas gave Marty a ride home, the bar had emptied out, save for the drooling heap at the bar. As they left, the bartender was calling Peyton Crane a cab.

CHAPTER EIGHTEEN
Sun Ceremony

THE FIRST HOOK was the most difficult. She had worn latex gloves, something she'd had stored out in the garage for when she didn't want her hands to get dirty while grooming. But, even so, touching the man's white skin revolted her. She had expected him to wake up once the first hook pierced the skin, but when he started bucking and trying to scream, she was nearly thrown clear off the bed. But Shawna had used plenty of rope to tie him to the bed, all those different knots Elmer had once taught her finally coming in handy. The duct tape over the mouth had been the last thing she'd had to do and it was the one thing that made her feel like some kind of serial killer. But she was glad now that she had. Peyton Crane was screaming for all he was worth, the veins in his forehead bulging something fierce. And, still, Shawna had trouble feeling much pity for the writhing, wailing lump of fat on the bed.

She pinched the flesh on his back together and inserted

another hook. Which wasn't exactly easy. Skin, in general, was tough. Fat or otherwise. And the fish hooks all had barbs on them. This didn't matter so much going in, but every time the idiot squirmed or bucked, they would chew into him, causing more of a mess. His back was already dripping with blood, the lines crisscrossing back and forth like an intricate web. It looked, Shawna found herself thinking vaguely, like an abstract painting.

A couple more hooks ought to do it and then she would try to hoist him up off the bed a few inches. A delicate task. One, the hooks could very well just tear out. This wasn't a young, slim, muscular and beautiful Chippewa boy after all. Which was why she'd decided to use so many hooks. It was about physics, surface area and tension. But even if the hooks did hold, there was no telling if the ceiling fan would. She had gotten lucky there, having had no other plan in mind if there wasn't something to string him up by. Her plan B was to simply hook him anyway and then pull on the strings herself. Even getting in had been easy since the moron had left the back door unlocked. And tying him up hadn't been too tough, either, since he'd been passed out drunk. Something Shawna had been counting on due to months of tracking his schedule, but she had brought the spear as backup just in case. And she'd made sure the kid wasn't there. This, too, she knew beforehand due to her back-porch stalking.

"I was going to put seven hooks into you, sort of like a tribute to Seven, but I didn't realize how fat you were. Good thing I brought a few extra lures."

The great white pig squirmed and moaned, his eyes bulging from his swollen face. The smell was bitter and acrid, like the very smell of hatred itself was seeping out of the man's skin. Shawna dug another hook in.

"Your best friend killed my mother. And now you've killed my best friend. And don't think I didn't consider poisoning you. That would have been fitting. If you ask me, you're getting off easy here."

She pinched another chunk of skin, wrestled the final hook into his skin and took a step back to consider her work. His body reminded her of a deer's after being skinned. Only way less elegant. She bent down beside his face. "By the way, what I'm doing to you is something boys used to do to themselves voluntarily. It was considered a rite of passage into manhood. It was a way to prove themselves. So, I guess instead of whining constantly, maybe you could try to see it that way. You see, real men don't swagger and bully. They are still and quiet until they are required to no longer be still and quiet."

With that, Shawna stood and grabbed the ropes, cinching them together through a steel ring she had taken off one of Seven's old halters. Attached to the other end of the ring was a longer, thicker lead rope that Shawna had already swung up and over the fairly large, and hopefully sturdy, ceiling fan. As she pulled, watching the smaller ropes go taut, it reminded her of walking back a kite, the man's skin like a billowing sail readying itself for lift-off. Only this kite wasn't going anywhere. She pulled the ropes tighter, the hooks now beginning to tear and stretch the skin. As she did this, the duct-taped squeals intensified.

"It feel like you're entering any kind of manhood yet? No? Okay, hold on a sec."

Shawna pulled on the rope again, slowly, so as not to tear her handiwork out, and again the skin stretched out gruesomely. Almost comically. Like one of those toys kids used to have where the arms and legs would stretch out. Elastic Man? She couldn't remember the name now. She pulled some more, having to lean her weight into it now, all the while eyeing the ceiling fan which seemed to be straining just as much as the man's skin. She stopped. The body, or at least the chest, was now clear of the bed sheets. Hovering. She opened a closet door, walking the rope back hand over hand so as not to let him drop back down, and managed to tie it to the knob. By the time she had finished, sweat was dripping from her face. As for Peyton Crane, he was quiet. And still. So much so that Shawna worried he'd passed out.

"You awake? I wouldn't want you to miss out on any of this. You want to earn your man-badge, don't you?"

But Peyton Crane wasn't passed out. He was wide awake, every inch of his insides shivering and trembling like a tuning fork. When he'd first woken up, he thought maybe it was Annette, his ex-wife, biting his back. After the divorce she'd gotten into some pretty kinky stuff, things they'd never even remotely done while married. Which, coincidentally, all began after she started seeing some dickhead down at the paper mill who was twenty years younger than Peyton. Not that it mattered much since she still came around, usually after breaking up with this new fella. And then out would come all the new tricks she'd learned. Most of which Peyton didn't care much for. And, hell, if she'd wanted him to hurt her so bad, he would have been more than happy to oblige her while they were still married.

But Annette wasn't in the room now. That girl was, the one with the damn horse he'd taken care of. Somebody must've seen and told her. Or maybe he'd said something at the bar while he was drunk. He could feel his skin stretching and tearing every time he so much as shivered. It was like the bitch had put meat hooks into him. He pulled on the rope tying his hands to the bed. If he could just get one hand free, it would be over in seconds. And then this girl could go join her horse in the sweet hereafter. Or wherever it was the dumbasses believed they went. But the rope wasn't giving any. And every time he so much as strained against it, he could feel whatever was in his back digging its teeth in further.

"I'm gonna get a beer. Want one?"

He could hear the girl open the fridge, her dirty little hands pawing away in there among his food. He'd have to toss everything once this was over with. He could see her feet as she came back into the room. Black boots. If he could speak, he'd ask her where her moccasins were. The sound of a can opening shot through the room making him flinch.

"That scare you? Sorry. Don't worry, I don't plan on shooting you or anything."

He listened as she drank, his beer travelling down her throat into her red belly. It angered him more than the hell she was putting his back through. She walked over to the side of the bed and just stood there. One good lunge and he could bite her thigh, but there was no telling what the meat hooks would do to him. Bite back, no doubt, but only worse.

"I didn't think it was possible to make a beer any shittier than Budweiser, but you've somehow managed to do it."

If he could get his teeth into her, he wouldn't let go.

"I'm being rude, though. Here, you should have some."

He felt the cold pour over his back. It was funny, but the beer actually felt okay. Almost like a salve. And, when he let his head hang down, some of it dribbled its way along his neck and then around the duct tape. He'd been poking his tongue out against it, seeing if there was any give to it.

"I don't know how you people can drink this swill. We injuns may not be able to handle our liquor, but if we had white money and jobs, we sure as shit would be smart enough to buy better booze."

The girl disappeared from his view, probably sitting at his desk in the corner of the room. The thought of her reading his private mail, or maybe looking through his computer, was too much. It nauseated him more than the blood he could now see pooling up on the sheets beneath him. Peyton breached his back and lowered his head so that his cheek was now touching the bed. He began to slowly move his head back and forth, brushing the tape against the bottom sheet. He could feel a slight peeling along one corner, the sweat and beer loosening it like he'd hoped. Just a little more and he'd have enough of it off so he could breathe. And, more importantly, speak. He arched his back and then lurched his head forward, dragging it across the bed, but, as he did, he felt a tearing along his back, the sound like somebody ripping cardboard in half. Then his body dropped a few inches on his right side. The pain of it came out in a half-gurgle half-scream, a sound not all that different from the one his wife had made when giving birth to their son.

"What have you done? Are you out of your mind?"

"You're Shawna Reynolds."

"And you're your own brand of idiot, you know that? You realize you ripped one of them out? And for what? So you could tell me my name? Brilliant."

"I know who you are. Guess now you'll be spending some time in jail with your step daddy. So who's the idiot?"

"Who says you'll be able to tell anyone?"

"You don't have the balls for that. None of your people do."

"Guess we'll find out, won't we?"

Peyton knew he needed something to rile her, something that might make her do something stupid. "Hey, you know what Martin's nickname was for your momma? Red Lobster. You wanna know why? Because all the white trashers liked to eat there."

He'd landed one. He could tell because she'd moved away from the bed and was now mumbling something to herself. This was his chance. Better to gain a few scars than end up dying in a pool of his own mess. But, then, just as he was beginning to strain against the ropes, intent on ripping out chunks of skin if need be to gain some slack, the oddest thing happened: she began to lower him back down. He grit his teeth and kept as still as possible, each little drop threatening to tear more pieces from his body.

Before long he was resting his head on the bed and could feel the hooks being removed from his skin, the sensation of which reminded him of a wet knife being slid from a sheath. After the last of the hooks had been removed, the girl lying them on the bed beside him as she took them out so he could see what she'd done, he could feel something dripping onto his back. But it wasn't beer this time.

The girl was crying.

"Knew you wouldn't kill me. Yours is a weak people. More gullible then even them dumb-ass Jews."

The girl stood up, the tears suddenly stopping.

"You know, I visit Martin just about once every week. He has the most incredible stories."

He could see the girl going into the kitchen, so he waited. What he was going to tell her wasn't true. Not at all. Martin had long since found religion and refused to take visits from Peyton anymore. No reason the girl had to know any of that, though.

"He loves talking about your mommy. You know, the day it all went down?"

The girl kept quiet and out of view. Which was unnerving. And he was getting weak from the loss of blood. He grabbed the ropes tying his hands together and sat up on his elbows. It probably wouldn't do much, but it was worth a shot.

"He likes to talk about what she looked like, you know, without any head. He said it was like the Fourth of July, only her head was the firework. What did he call it now? *Blooming Red Blossom.* Or something like that anyway. Said it was the most beautiful thing he'd ever seen. Even the cops were all like *ooh* and *aww.*"

Peyton Crane gave one big yank and, much to his surprise, managed to crack the top of the bed frame where the girl had secured the rope. He hurriedly went about untying his hands, grinning all the while at the prospect of soon getting his hands around the girl's throat. Then, just as he was nearly free, he saw the girl standing there over him, her eyes burning, then the blunt end of the spear coming down as he recognized the yellow lure dangling from her ear as his own.

That's my girl.

When it was done, Shawna dropped the spear and sat on the floor holding her knees, rocking back and forth. She wanted to look at what she'd done but couldn't because she was shaking so horribly. The room was quiet now. That was the important thing. She needed to gather up all the ropes and lures and put them in her bag. She'd watched enough crime shows to know that her DNA was going to be found one way or another, so she wasn't worried about that. She just didn't want to leave a mess. Aside from the human one on the bed.

Now run and hide yourself.

Shawna covered her ears and stood, forcing herself to look at the man on the bed. He was so still. His head wasn't caved in like she feared, though there was a dark wet spot above his forehead. She couldn't tell if he was breathing or not, but she wasn't going to get any closer to find out.

She grabbed her bag, a few more beers, and an entire rotisserie chicken from the fridge that looked like it hadn't been touched yet. The sun would be coming up soon. As she got in her car, a few layers of dark seemed to have already peeled away.

Hurry.

Shawna started the car and looked in the backseat.

She knew she'd brought the headlamp for a reason.

CHAPTER NINETEEN
The Scamp

KAY DID HAVE secrets. Although they weren't the same kind of secrets her husband and his poems had. Kay's were a little duller, or on a smaller scale maybe, but once she got started writing them down she found she couldn't stop. And with every little secret she put down, she felt herself growing a little bit lighter, and, simultaneously, a little bit less empty. Once she'd finished, she realized that her biggest secret was maybe that she had been happy and content in her life. And she wanted that secret for Douglas, too.

"Thank you for doing this, Alma."

"You got me out of babysitting duty, so, trust me, I don't mind."

"I thought you adored little Jovie."

"Oh, I do, but the girl never stops talking. It's like one constant stream of thought. By the time they come to get her, my ears are literally ringing sometimes."

"Just be happy you're not hearing things."

"What kind of things are you hearing?"

"Norm, sometimes, but it's just my mind playing tricks on me."

"Let's hope so."

"What does that mean?"

"You remember Daisy Lowell, the woman who lived two doors down from me?"

"But she was always a little off even before the dementia set in."

"True, but she used to tell me how she heard her dead husband following her around the house and complaining about this and that. She said the man wasn't satisfied with having made her miserable enough in this world, so he stayed around in the next one to make sure he finished the job."

"Well, Norm doesn't say anything mean."

"What does he say then?"

"Just the same old boring stuff he said when he was alive. *What's for dinner? Anything good on tonight? Have you seen my slippers? I'll take a look at it later.*"

Kay had asked her to meet her at the new coffee shop. She'd decided it was time to help Douglas help himself. The thought of him wasting away at home with her as she succumbed to whatever was heading her way was just too much to bear.

JENNA SET THEIR drinks down. Alma had ordered something called a latte. It seemed just about everyone was more sophisticated than Kay.

"Here you ladies are. I'll bring my laptop over in a minute and help you upload the photos. It shouldn't take that long."

"Are you sure it's not too much trouble?"

Jenna gestured to the nearly empty room. There was one other customer, a young person who hadn't once looked up from his phone since she and Alma came in. "I think I can spare a few minutes. It's for a worthy cause after all."

"He does have talent, doesn't he? You're not just humoring an old lady?"

"I don't play around when it comes to art. There's not much point. Douglas has something unique. That much I'm certain of. He just needs some help with the fine-tuning."

"And you think this school can do that?"

"If he puts the time in, which I know he will, then yes. It's one of the best out there."

Kay let out a deep sigh. "Okay, let's do this then."

Alma had brought her digital camera from home and went about taking pictures of Douglas's sketches. When she was done, Jenna sat down with them and attached the photos to the online application. It was something called a low-residency program where they held two-week workshops every semester in Green Bay. Kay could get Marty to watch the shop during those times. When they finally hit the send button, Kay felt close to tears.

"How long until we find out?"

Jenna scrolled through a few things. "Looks like we should know in about a week."

"And you think he'll get in?"

"I don't know. I've had friends apply to this program who didn't make the cut. It's a pretty big deal, but I'd say he has a decent shot."

"Well, no matter what happens, at least we tried. Thank you both for that."

MORE THAN A week had passed, and still Kay hadn't heard anything from the school. As a result, she was having trouble sleeping at night. At least that's what she was blaming it on. The night before she had gotten up to use the bathroom and had once again seen a light moving across the lake. Or, rather, a boat with someone holding a flashlight had been heading toward the island. There was only one person Kay knew of who would do such a thing, but she hadn't been willing to go out there at that hour to find out. Besides, people going to that sort of trouble no doubt wanted to be alone. Or with their significant other. Which was the last thing Kay wanted to interrupt. So, she had decided to wait until morning to investigate.

From the shore, Kay couldn't see the boat moored on the island, but she knew it was most likely there. She lugged one of the blue plastic kayaks into the water and climbed in from the dock. When she did, the damned thing hunkered down into the sand so that she had to scoot her bottom forward until she was actually floating.

Once she was paddling, a small breeze at her back feathered the surface of the water, putting her more at ease. After making it halfway to the island without too much effort, she let herself float a while, her body relaxing into the kayak and the surrounding quiet. As she neared the island, Kay could see the boat nestled there among the foxtails and reed grass. She dug the paddle deep into the water, giving one last solid push so that she and the kayak were able to run up onto the sand. "A little help?" she called out, hoping she was right and it *was* Shawna who had taken the boat and not some madman.

Kay was about to attempt to get herself out, something she had never quite managed without toppling herself into the water, when a ghost emerged from the trees.

A raccoon ghost.

"My lord, what happened to you?"

Shawna, her eyes and cheeks smudged with charcoal, stepped into the water to help Kay out. "I'm fine. It's just an Ojibwa thing."

When the girl didn't offer any more of an explanation, Kay decided to just go ahead and ask. "So is it a ceremony type thing? We Catholics have something called Ash Wednesday where I usually end up leaving the church looking a little like that."

There was a plastic crate on the island used as a seat for around the fire pit. Shawna turned it over for Kay to sit on and sat back down on her sleeping bag next to a half-eaten rotisserie chicken. She tore some off and offered it to Kay.

"No, thank you. I ate earlier." She hesitated, unsure of how to say what needed to be said. "I'm sorry about Seven. It's my fault he's dead. I know that doesn't help you at all, but I want you to know I feel like... like a garbage can because of it."

Shawna said nothing, only raised the leg of chicken in the air, pointing it at Kay to indicate she'd used the exact right word. Kay kept quiet, watched as the girl tore a hunk off with her teeth and began to chew it fiercely. There were streaks down her face, valleys carved out through the dirt and grime and whatever else she'd done to her face. She looked wounded to Kay. And frightened. Like a stray dog cowering with a scrap of meat it'd just found.

"Is that blood on your hands? Did you kill that chicken yourself?"

"It's from Snow's. I think."

"But is that blood? Honey, are you okay? You can talk to me, you know."

"I know." The girl took another bite of chicken, placing what was left back into the plastic bag. She then wiped her hands on her jeans. "It's not my blood." She looked up at Kay and, like she was concerned about Kay not under-standing, added, "Or the chicken's."

"I may be old, honey, but I'm not dim. Not yet, anyway. And last I checked, they don't sell live chickens down at Snow's."

The girl smiled briefly but then shook her head and covered her ears. *"She's okay,"* Kay heard the girl whisper through gritted teeth.

"Shawna...?"

"I'm fine."

"You're not fine."

"No. Maybe not."

Seeing as she wasn't getting anywhere with the girl, Kay decided to take a different approach. "Come to think of it, I am a little hungry. Could I have some, please?"

Shawna ripped a chunk of meat from the bone. "Could you tell me more about the choice of makeup?" Kay said, trying her best to seem like she was enjoying her meal. "I bet it's interesting."

Kay then listened as Shawna told her about Ojibwa death rituals and how when somebody dies they rub charcoal over the faces of children so the deceased won't recognize them and try to take them with them when they finally leave on their journey. Kay had a lot of questions about this but decided it was best to focus on keeping the girl talking. "But you aren't a child."

"I guess I was taking extra precautions. Stupid, I know."

"But why? Who died?"

"Nobody. I don't think so anyway."

"Shawna, tell me what happened."

The girl spoke about something called a Sun Ceremony and how it was a rite of passage into manhood for boys, how Shawna had always wanted to try it herself, to test herself, how it wasn't fair that only the boys got to do it. Then there was something about using fishing lures, and one she'd found on the island, which was now hanging from her ear, and that she was surprised how resilient human skin was. But throughout her talking, nowhere was there any actual mention of *who* had possibly died. When the girl finally stopped, Kay asked her again: "Who *maybe* died, Shawna?"

"He didn't die. He better not have."

"Who *didn't* die?"

The girl hesitated, wringing her hands and picking at pieces of dirt, or worse, blood, on her jeans and eyeing the bag of chicken like maybe it was going to run off. Then, just when Kay was about to give up, in a whisper the girl said, "Peyton Crane."

"That nasty man who had Seven?"

"He killed Seven. He even admitted it."

Kay looked at the girl and realized she was, in a way, looking at a ghost. If what the girl was saying were true, even if the man was still alive, she'd be going to prison. And after everything that had happened to this poor girl, how could she expect to come out of it unscathed? Or whole? As Kay looked at the girl, an enormous sadness overtook her. This world, she couldn't help thinking, was enough to crush just about anybody.

"But you're certain he's still alive?"

"I had Elmer go over and check on him."

"And what did Elmer say?"

"That he took care of him, bandaged him up and everything."

"And the police?"

"Elmer says he took care of that, too."

"How?"

"He just said he didn't think Peyton would ever say

anything about it to anybody. Partly because it was embarrassing. Me being a girl and all."

"And what's the other part?"

"I don't know. Elmer said he scared him pretty bad. Elmer can be scary when he wants to be."

"You need a shower. And some clean clothes. Will you come back to the house with me? We can figure out the rest later."

"I don't know," Shawna said, again eyeing the chicken like maybe Kay was trying to trick her out of it.

"And I'll make you BLTs until you never want to see another piece of bacon again. Deal?"

Shawna smiled, but it wasn't the same smile Kay had come to know. It was a shadow of the old one, a nervous thing being chased away as soon as it appeared. "We can take the rowboat back, but you're going to have to do the rowing. My arms are shot."

Together they gathered Shawna's things and loaded them into the boat. Kay sat in the back and held onto a rope attached to the kayak, towing it behind them. The lake was empty, just the two of them making their way across the water. Watching the girl work the oars, it seemed to Kay like they were both leaving a place they could never return to. It was just as she was thinking this that the Scamp, stuck there along the edge of the lake, came into view and the idea came to her.

"Do Chippewa believe in funeral pyres?"

Shawna guided the boat in and hooked them to the

side of the dock. "Not anymore really. After four days we bury them in a cemetery just like your people do."

"Norm is still in my living room."

"Why are you asking me?"

"I don't know. I just had an idea for something."

Shawna shrugged. "Do you mind if I take a raincheck on those BLTs. I think I just want to go home and shower and change. Maybe talk some with my naan."

"You do whatever you need to do. We can talk later."

With that, Kay watched as Shawna climbed the hill leading up to the house. She'd left the half-eaten chicken sitting there on the dock, so Kay carried it back up to the house and tossed it in the trash. The girl eating like that bothered Kay. She went inside and found the tin of old recipes on the kitchen table and tucked them into her jacket to give to her later. Then she got on the phone and started making calls.

Starting with Marty.

<hr />

MARTY DIDN'T KNOW exactly why Kay had asked to borrow his truck, only that she needed to use the winch to help say "goodbye to the past." He'd called Douglas down at the shop immediately afterward and, after getting the okay, made plans to meet him and Jenna at the house.

In the front yard stood Kay, another old woman, and a priest. Which sounded to Marty like the start of a bad joke.

Kay introduced Marty to her friend Alma and Father Jason. While Alma and the Father chatted about the recent Packers game, Kay took Marty aside and pointed down at the Scamp.

"You think you can haul that thing up the hill about halfway?"

"I can try. We'll need to put some chocks of wood behind my wheels, so I don't roll down after it. Why only halfway?"

"I want to send it rolling back down into the lake. Then I want to set it on fire."

"You're kidding."

"The Father here is even going to bless it."

"You do realize that's totally illegal, right? Not to mention your neighbors will call the cops before it even hits water."

"But we're still doing it."

"And Douglas knows about this?"

"No, not yet. But he won't mind."

"Doesn't he hang out in there and draw and stuff?"

"It's been overrun by Gypsy moths. And the law says they need to be destroyed. So..."

"You could just spray."

"No, way too many of them. This is better. Plus, Douglas needs to stop hiding."

Marty knew from experience that it was pretty much useless to try to change Kay's mind once she had it set on something. And chances were they'd just give her a fine.

Either way, not Marty's problem. "I'll have to drag it a little across the lawn so it'll clear the trees. It might do some collateral damage. That okay?"

"I don't care about the grass. Just be sure you don't mess with Douglas's steps. He spent a lot of time on them."

"I'll stay clear of them. Don't worry about that."

"Good. And thank you, Marty."

"We'll see how happy you are once Mercer's finest shows up."

"Oh, they don't scare me. Besides, I can always blame it on the Alzheimer's." She made a funny face at Marty, like someone lost in a big city, and he laughed out loud though he didn't want to.

"Douglas told me about that. I'm sorry, Mrs. O."

"Nothing to be sorry about. At least I have a little time to get things in order before I disappear. And you're helping me, aren't you? That's what this is all about. Saying goodbye to things, putting them to rest. Which reminds me, I'll be needing you to put in more hours down at the shop soon. You'll be more or less running the place for a bit. Is that something that might interest you?"

"Definitely. I'd be honored, Mrs. O."

"Good. We can talk more about it later then. Oh, and would you want Norm's fishing rod? Douglas won't ever use it, and it'd be nice to know it was getting some use. You could think of it as payment for helping us today."

Marty was about to mention that Douglas had already offered the rod to him, but he didn't want to ruin the gesture she was trying to make. "That would be really nice, Mrs. O. Thank you."

"Good, I'm glad. I'll be sure to grab it for you later."

Kay watched as Marty went about getting the truck in position, securing it as best he could with a few stray logs from what was left of their firewood. There was maybe an eighth of a cord left. She'd have to remember to check with Douglas about ordering more before winter set in.

Satisfied things were going according to plan, she went inside to grab the urn from off the top of the TV.

"You sure about that?" Alma said, walking over to her.

"Norm loved the lake."

"Yeah, but he also loved TV."

"Honestly, I don't think it matters much either way. I'm just tired of looking at it."

"It's up to you. And I don't want to sound cruel here, but eventually, you're not going to know whose ashes those are anyway."

Kay laughed, mainly because there was nothing else she could do, and placed the urn back on the TV. She thought about the list of secrets she'd made or maybe the recipes as worthy sacrifices, but, instead, she grabbed the Don Quixote statue from off the coffee table. "Okay, Norm can stay. I guess maybe the bottom of a lake isn't such an ideal resting spot after all."

Kay went outside to keep the priest company; he was standing there watching Marty work, his toes wriggling about in his sandals happy as could be. "This is going into the Scamp. You want to say goodbye to anything of yours, Father?"

"Hmmm, let me see. Can I put my tinnitus in?"

"I didn't know you had problems with your ears."

"Just these past few months. I have to use earplugs during my sermons now when the organ gets going."

"Or when Lucy Dilmore gets going."

The priest wagged a finger at Kay. "You're a funny one, Kay. But I happen to think Lucy is a fine singer."

"I think that might make you a saint then, Father. Either that or your tinnitus is worse than you think."

Kay walked down to the Scamp, eased open the door, and slid the statue in. "Nothing personal," she whispered. "You were the poet he always wanted to be. And I don't want to be reminded of that anymore." There had to be hundreds of moths, maybe thousands, in there by now. Had she not known better, she would have thought the Scamp was filled with bats by all the racket they were making in there.

When she climbed back up the steps to the house, she saw Douglas and Jenna pulling in. As she passed by the priest again on her way into the house, Kay decided that if there ever was a time to say something, now was it. "You know, Father, we can throw your sandals in there, too, if you'd like. Don't you think it might be time to put them to rest?"

Father Jason looked down at his feet. "My sandals? What's wrong with my sandals?"

"Nothing's *wrong* with them. I've just heard people talking is all."

"Fine, I'll bite. What are people saying?"

"Oh, just that maybe sandals aren't befitting a man of the cloth."

"Befitting?"

"Well, they're not exactly holy-looking, are they?"

"You do realize who else was fond of wearing sandals, right?"

Kay hadn't considered this before, but, solid as his point was, she wasn't about to let that distract her from her mission. "Well, maybe he had nicer-looking feet."

"What's wrong with my feet now?"

"Nothing at all, Father. I shouldn't have even brought it up."

The priest curled his toes under like he was trying to make them disappear. "No, I'm glad you told me. Maybe they are a bit much."

"We can't all be Jesus. If it's any consolation, I know the ladies who count the donation money think you walk on water."

"Only when necessary."

"Another joke. Good for you, Father." Kay, whether she wanted to or not, was starting to like the man. And who was she to tell him what to wear? "I'm going in to fix a drink. Can I get you one?"

"I would like that. Thank you, Catherine."

She found Douglas inside making Jenna and himself a

sandwich. She hadn't seen him as much as she'd have liked to lately, so it was extra good having him there.

"Have you told him what we've been up to yet?"

"Not a word."

"Good girl."

Douglas took a bite of his sandwich and, with his mouth full, muttered, "I already don't like this. Whatever it is."

"We decided you're going to art school." Kay could tell Douglas was about to make a big stink about it, so she skipped right to the selling point. "It's an online course, so you can do it from home."

Jenna, without so much as a nod from Kay, took up the baton. "You'll only go to classes for two weeks out of every semester."

"And Marty has already agreed to take on more responsibilities at the shop."

"God help us."

"You know he's more than capable, Douglas. Your father made sure of that."

Jenna slid her arm through Douglas's, pulled him to her. "It's a great school. I'd go if I had the money. And it's a pretty big deal if you get in."

"He got in."

"Baby, that's great!" When Douglas stiffened, Jenna eased away from him a little. "I mean if you decide to go, of course."

Douglas looked like he was in shock. Either that, or

irritated to the point of paralysis. Kay couldn't decide which it was. "But how did you...?"

"Alma helped. And so did this wonderful lady."

"And the money for it? Where does that come from?"

"I've already spoken with a loan officer. We'll be able to figure something out." When Douglas still seemed unsure of what to think, Kay added, "Please. Do it for your old mother if you aren't smart enough to do it for yourself."

"Marty and I have been talking and the Scamp probably won't make it out too far if we just let it go as is. But don't worry, we have a plan."

"Douglas."

"Fine. So the school sounds good. I don't know what to say, honestly."

Jenna nudged him. "Say thank you."

"Thank you. Everybody. I mean that."

Kay kissed him on his cheek right there in front of everyone, and Douglas didn't seem to mind. It was one of the things she loved about him. He had never once acted like he was embarrassed of her no matter what she did.

Douglas, no doubt wanting to take the focus off himself, said, "I was serious about the Scamp, though. Remember those old inner tubes I got a few summers ago for the lake?"

"They're still taking up half of our shed if I remember correctly."

"We can tie them to the bottom of the Scamp. That way when it hits the water, it'll float out a bit more. Well, hopefully. What's wrong? I thought you'd love that idea."

"It's not that. It's a wonderful idea."

"So what's wrong then?"

"There's something else I need to talk to you about." She looked over at Alma, and Alma nodded before asking Jenna if she'd like to meet Father Jason. Once they were alone, Kay told Douglas everything she could remember about what Shawna had told her.

"Have you called the police?"

"No."

"Well, that's good, I guess. As long as we're sure he's okay."

"Shawna says Elmer thinks he'll be fine in a week or two. I don't know, though."

"What a nightmare. I'll go check on her in a minute."

"Is there anything you want to put in the Scamp before it's time?"

After thinking a minute, Douglas said, "Yeah, maybe. Hold on."

He went to his room and returned with a sheet of paper. On it was a pencil drawing of his father climbing a flight of stairs, a fishing pole in his hand being used as a cane. The stairs led up into a sky filled with dark, ominous-looking clouds.

"You sure you want to part with this?"

"I'm sure."

"I hope this means you're letting it go and forgiving yourself. Even though there's really nothing to forgive."

"I guess. Something like that, anyway."

"Well, good. Now I better get a stiff drink out to Father before he tries to convert Jenna."

"Good luck with that."

"Oh, one more thing. I want to set it on fire once we launch it. Any ideas on how we do that?"

Douglas took a bite of his sandwich and, with his mouth full, said, "I might have one."

As Douglas headed over to Shawna's, he didn't have a clue what he was going to say. *Hey, sorry to hear you nearly killed someone. Wanna come over and light a camper on fire with us?* When he got there, though, he found Shawna sitting with Elmer next to a pile of Seven's blankets.

"Hey. Hey, Elmer." Shawna looked different to Douglas. Like somebody had sucked out whatever it was that made Shawna Shawna and left her there all hollowed out. "Can you tell me what happened?"

She looked at Douglas, and immediately he wanted to hold her. She looked frightened. And he'd never really seen her look scared before. "I screwed up is all. Nothing new."

"I don't know what to say. Do you think he's okay?"

"Has your mom called the police?"

"No. She wouldn't do that."

"I guess it really doesn't matter much either way. I don't care what happens to me anymore. I'm just done, you know?"

Douglas had felt that way after his dad died. Or thought he had felt that way. But, obviously, this was a whole different kind of *done*. "Didn't you go check on him, Elmer? How'd he seem to you?"

Elmer shrugged. "Not good."

"Well, yeah. I'm guessing he wasn't looking his Sunday best."

"Elmer went over there with his dad. His dad is sort of like the Chippewa version of Peyton Crane."

"Hey."

"Well, he is. He's a drunk, and he hates white people."

Elmer shrugged again and pulled out a pack of cigarettes. "My dad talked to him, explained to him what would happen if he said a word to the police."

"And you think he'll keep quiet?"

"I know he'll keep quiet."

Douglas was quiet for a bit. He wasn't sure he wanted to know exactly why Elmer was so sure. In the end, it didn't matter so long as Shawna was safe. When Elmer got up and started putting the blankets in the shed, Douglas stopped him. "So I know this is kind of weird, but we're going to launch our Scamp into the lake tonight and then try to set it on fire. We're all putting things inside that we want to say goodbye to. Would you want to put one of those blankets in? Sort of like a burial kind of thing?"

"Can I put myself in?" Shawna said, taking a drag off Elmer's cigarette, something Douglas had never seen her do before.

"I don't think my mom would go for that. Or the priest that's there."

"That's a shame." She looked down at the blankets Elmer was holding. "Sure, why not?"

"Okay, good. And you should bring your bow and arrows. Would you be up for that? It might be therapeutic."

Shawna shrugged. "Why not?" Her voice sounded bottomless, like you could drop a coin down into it and never hear the splash. She took the topmost blanket from Elmer and handed it to Douglas before going into the garage for the bow. When she came back, Shawna walked up to Douglas and said, "Do you believe in spirits?"

"I don't know," he said, thinking of the loon and what she'd said about spirits traveling from bigger to smaller animals. "Maybe."

"I do," she said. "I believe in spirits."

For a second, he thought maybe she was going to tell him something, something that would make sense out of everything, but instead she and Elmer just started off towards his house. The words *My dad died* came into his head, but it seemed almost laughable now. How small of a thing it was to say. How ridiculously selfish.

Once Shawna had tossed the blanket in the Scamp, she grabbed a shiny pamphlet of some sort from her back pocket, but Elmer stopped her before she could throw it inside. Instead, she removed one of her earrings and threw that in. When Douglas set about dousing the inside of the Scamp with gasoline, he saw the earring there on the floor. It was a yellow fishing lure. He didn't know much about lures, but it looked like an old one to him, something bulky and made from wood that people no longer used much. When Douglas finished, Marty took the can from him and emptied what was left onto the roof.

"This is nuts. Do you think it'll actually work?"

"No, but if it makes Mom happy..."

Marty jumped down and together they tied two of the inner tubes, one on each side, to the bottom of the Scamp. It seemed much larger to Douglas now, almost like a small ship they'd be launching into the water.

"That should do it. Even if it doesn't work, we're going to see a show."

"A shit show," Marty said, taking the steps back up to the house. He stopped a minute and nudged a piece of rebar with his boot. "You did a nice job on these, by the way. Norm would have liked them."

"Yeah, thanks. Maybe he would have."

Kay was waiting at the top of the hill with a drink in hand, watching the living room windows pulse with TV light.

This could be any night.

Norm could be in there.

She studied Douglas's steps, how they curved and meandered down the hill. When Douglas and Marty reached the top, she suggested they christen them.

"The steps?"

"Sure."

"Okay by me. But don't we need champagne or something?"

"I think Jim Beam will suffice, don't you? To Norm," Kay said and poured some of her drink onto the steps. "May he always have Paris." She then turned to Father Jason and asked him to bless the Scamp before they sent it down the hill. The priest dutifully raised his glass to the camper.

"Let us pray that everything dear you hold inside will find the peace it so surely deserves. Amen!"

Kay, trying not to laugh, motioned for Marty to get ready to release their hostage.

"On the count of three. Everybody now... One, two, three!"

With that Marty disengaged the clutch on the winch, letting the cable unspool, sending the Scamp rolling down the hill. There was a gap between the birch trees wide enough to fit two campers through, but the Scamp only just managed to squeeze by, the side of it scraping bark from the trees as it hurtled past into the water where it immediately capsized, turning on its side with the door now facing the sky. But the inner tubes had managed to do their work, and the Scamp was floating now, lopsided as it was, out toward the center of the lake.

Kay patted Father Jason on the back. "Cripes, it actually worked."

"Oh, ye of little faith. I knew it would all along."

"C'mon, Father. We aren't finished yet."

Kay looked over at Shawna, wanting to say something to her that would give her some peace, but she knew there were no words for such a thing. Instead, she quietly grabbed her hand and held it as they all walked down to the dock with the sun setting on the other side of the lake. Everyone remained quiet as Shawna handed Douglas the bow.

"This is all you."

"But..."

"But nothing. I'll help you."

Shawna set one of the arrows in the bow, then guided Douglas's arm so that he was on target. She then lit the end of one of the arrows, and, from behind, helped Douglas pull the bowstring back. She whispered something in his ear, and he nodded, aiming the arrow a touch higher before sending it up into the air. The arrow missed, though, sputtering out safely in the water a few feet shy of the Scamp.

"Maybe setting it on fire isn't such a good idea," Kay said to no one in particular.

"No, we can do this."

Shawna loaded the bow again and, when Douglas was ready, lit another sock. Douglas's arm was shaking, but this time the arrow landed squarely on the side of the Scamp, flames quickly crawling up and over the camper. Everyone stood around quietly, reverently, watching as the Scamp lit up the lake, creating something like a floating bonfire. Neighbors on the other side soon came out of their houses to watch. And while Kay couldn't be sure, she thought she could see moths billowing out through the open door along with the smoke, turning to embers as they floated skyward.

Then, just as Kay was wondering if the moths were suffering, if she were no better than Norm abandoning all those poor fish in the bait box, colored lights came flashing and rolling through the trees behind them. Two squad cars pulled into their driveway.

"Is that for us?" Marty said. "How could they have found out so quickly?"

"They couldn't have," Douglas said. "Let me go see what they want."

"Looks like they're coming to us," Kay said, grabbing her son's hand, preparing for the worst.

"Throwing yourselves a little party here?" Officer Christopher said once he reached the dock, two other officers behind him. "Mind if I ask what the occasion is?"

Douglas, out of habit from dealing with him down at the shop, was the one to respond. "No party. We just had a little accident."

"So you accidentally set fire to that structure in the water?"

"Well, no, but we were trying to tow our camper away when it came loose and ended up there in the water."

"Why's it floating then?"

Marty, not about to miss out on the fun, said, "That's because of the inner tubes, Chris. We were trying to protect the bottom from getting damaged. As you can see, that didn't quite work out."

"And that?" Officer Christopher said, pointing to the bow hanging at Douglas's side.

When Douglas didn't seem to have any explanation, Kay took the bow from him. "That camper is infested with gypsy moths. We were going to dispose of it properly, but once it got loose, we thought this might be the easiest solution. You should give us a medal, seeing how many of those damn things we just torched."

Officer Christopher shook his head. "Well, lucky for you, that's not what we're here for. You mind if I take a look at that bow you've got? And one of those arrows while you're at it?"

Douglas glanced back at Shawna who was standing directly behind his mom. As far as he knew, she hadn't used the bow and arrow on Peyton Crane. "Sure," he mumbled and handed it over.

"Everybody, just stay put now. This won't take long."

Officer Christopher motioned to one of the other officers who then handed him a plastic bag. Inside the bag was a burnt arrow. A light was shined on the bag, then on Shawna's bow and arrow, and back again to the bag. After some whispering among the three, Officer Christopher turned his light on the group, shining it directly in one face and then another, before stopping on Shawna's.

"Are you Shawna Reynolds by any chance?"

Shawna stepped forward. "I'm Shawna Reynolds."

"And this here is your bow?"

"It is."

"We received an anonymous tip and believe you may be the one responsible for the destruction of the town loon. We'll be taking you down to the station now for questioning. Do you understand?"

"I understand."

Stand tall, girl. We are warriors. Don't ever forget that.

Shawna pulled the brochure from her back pocket and handed it to Elmer. "Sorry."

"Don't be. I didn't like that place anyway."

"Yes, you did."

"We can still go, Shawna. Maybe we just have to wait a little."

"Will you talk to my naan? Just don't bring her down there tonight. She's already seen enough police stations."

Elmer nodded and Officer Christopher motioned for one of the officers to take Shawna up to the squad car. "Be sure to read her her rights."

Douglas looked over at his mom who seemed just as relieved as he was. Which made what he was about to do all that much easier. "I helped."

Officer Christopher took a step toward Douglas. "You'll want to be very careful right now."

"I was there. I helped her. I lit the arrows."

Officer Christopher shook his head. "What about Burning Woman there?" he said, motioning toward Jenna. "She help, too?"

"No. Just me."

"Okay, have it your way."

Douglas turned to Jenna and his mom. "I'm sorry. But I was there, you know?"

Jenna didn't say anything but, instead, simply put her arm around Kay's shoulders. Douglas, though, could tell Jenna wasn't fazed much by what was happening. His mom, too, seemed pretty coolheaded. Maybe, after everything that had happened lately, Douglas and Shawna about to climb into the back of a police car didn't quite rank up there with the end of the world as it once might have.

"It's okay," Kay said quietly. "We'll see you down there soon."

"So," Marty said, following after the officers as they started up the steps. "Seeing as Norm was such an upstanding member of the community and everything, maybe you guys could give them a break?" When Officer Christopher didn't respond, Marty added, "Unless, of course, you want all those unpaid shop receipts Norm kept over the years to find their way to *The Daily Globe*."

Officer Christopher stopped and, for once, turned to address Marty head on. "And who do you suppose would pay for the damage then?"

"By my calculations, the city's already been paid," Marty said evenly. "And then some."

Officer Thomas stared off over Marty's head at the lake, the temple in his forehead visibly throbbing. "Fine. Douglas can go."

Marty took another step forward. "Shawna, too. She's like family. To them, I mean."

After a few seconds, Officer Thomas turned and mumbled something to the other officers before turning to Kay.

"I'm going to let this one slide, Mrs. O'Brien. But I don't want to see anything sticking out of that lake come morning. Do we understand one another?"

"All you'll see is some lovely morning fog," Kay said and smiled at Marty. "That's a promise."

Once the police had gone, Kay invited everyone up to the house for a nightcap. If there had ever been a time to celebrate, she figured, now was it. "I'm going to get Norm's fishing pole for you before I forget," she told Marty as the group headed inside. "It's the least I could do." Marty began to protest, but Kay wasn't having it. Besides, she knew right where the pole was. After the ambulance took

Norm away, she had put it back where he'd always kept it, just inside the tin door of the shack. After she'd found the pole, Kay hesitated there by the dock, staring out at the now smoldering Scamp. She thought about Seven, hoping that he forgave her and that his spark had turned to flame and was now racing through the heavens. Something then flashed in the water near the bait box, and she couldn't help but imagine a sunfish caught in there. A giant one. With a hole in its side.

She stood there, waiting for what, exactly, she didn't know. Maybe she was waiting for Norm's voice, for him to apologize for never telling her about the poetry, to tell her that he was sorry she was losing her mind. But all she could hear was a loon keening away somewhere out in the dark. She looked up at the yellow glow of the kitchen window and the people standing there, then at the new steps, at the way they swam and eddied like a stream down the hill, the way they pushed out against their borders and fanned and widened as they approached the dock. Like they were lost and trying to find their way.

Sign up for new releases at www.jamiezerndt.com .

THE KOREAN WORD FOR BUTTERFLY

SET AGAINST THE backdrop of the 2002 World Cup and rising anti-American sentiment due to a deadly accident involving two young Korean girls and a U.S. tank, The Korean Word For Butterfly is told from three alternating points-of-view:

Billie, the young wanna-be poet looking for adventure with her boyfriend who soon finds herself questioning her decision to travel so far from the comforts of American life;

Moon, the ex K-pop band manager who now works at the English school struggling to maintain his sobriety in hopes of getting his family back;

And Yun-ji , a secretary at the school whose new feelings of resentment toward Americans may lead her to do something she never would have imagined possible.

The Korean Word For Butterfly is a story about the choices we make and why we make them.

It is a story, ultimately, about the power of love and redemption.

THE ROADRUNNER CAFÉ

ONE YEAR AFTER his father's suicide, Carson Long feels cheated. He hates his father for leaving him and his sister, Georgie, alone. He hates him for turning his mother into a young widow who hasn't left the house in months. And he hates his father for leaving behind his stupid tree. Four of them are planted outside the restaurant, one for each family member. That is until Carson's mother, no longer able to stand the sight of the tree, hires a local landscaper to remove it in the middle of the night. This seemingly unremarkable act soon sets in motion of series of events in the small Colorado ski town that leaves more than just young Carson groping in the dark for answers.

The Roadrunner Café is a unique novel told from multiple points of view about loss and the lengths some will go to heal the human heart. Ultimately, it is a story about what it takes to go on living even when everything in the world might be telling us it isn't possible to.

*Intended for adults and mature teens. Contains some profanity and violence.

THE CLOUD SEEDERS

Serve Your Country, Conserve Your Water, Observe Your Neighbor

THIS IS THE slogan of the Sustainability Unit and of a country gone eco-hysterical. After nearly twelve months without rain and the hinges of the world barely still oiled, Thomas and his younger brother, Dustin, set out across a drought-ridden landscape in search of answers. What they discover along the way will change their lives, and their country, forever. *The Cloud Seeders* weaves humor and heartache, as well as poetry and science, into a unique crossover novel that defies categorization.

EVERYONE'S HAPPIER THAN YOU

A COLLECTION OF short poems from over the years, a handful of which have previously appeared in places like Edgar Literary Review, Sow's Ear Poetry Review, Nerve Cowboy, and The Oregonian Newspaper.

Chapbook length: approximately 50 poems

Note: Some of these poems appear in *The Cloud Seeders*

THE TREE POACHERS AND OTHER STORIES

A COLLECTION OF short stories, a few of which were the seeds for later novels. Some of these have appeared in such publications as Gray's Sporting Journal, SWINK magazine, and Revolver.

Note: Chapbook length, approximately 150 pages. Contains adult language/themes.